D1013704

THE ROCK STAR
IN SEAT 3A

Also by Jill Kargman

Fiction

Arm Candy

The Ex-Mrs. Hedgefund

Momzillas

Wolves in Chic Clothing: A Novel (with Carrie Karasyov)

The Right Address: A Novel (with Carrie Karasyov)

Nonfiction

Sometimes I Feel Like a Nut

Children's Fiction

Pirates and Princesses

Kargman, Jill, 1974-
The rock star in seat 3A /
2013, ©2012.
3330525099452
gi   04/04/22

THE ROCK STAR
IN SEAT 3A

Jill Kargman

WILLIAM MORROW
An Imprint of HarperCollinsPublishers

This book is a work of fiction. The characters, incidents, and dialogue are drawn from the author's imagination and are not to be construed as real. Any resemblance to actual events or persons, living or dead, is entirely coincidental.

THE ROCK STAR IN SEAT 3A. Copyright © 2012 by Pirates and Princesses. All rights reserved. Printed in the United States of America. No part of this book may be used or reproduced in any manner whatsoever without written permission except in the case of brief quotations embodied in critical articles and reviews. For information address HarperCollins Publishers, 10 East 53rd Street, New York, NY 10022.

HarperCollins books may be purchased for educational, business, or sales promotional use. For information please write: Special Markets Department, HarperCollins Publishers, 10 East 53rd Street, New York, NY 10022.

A hardcover edition of this book was published in 2012 by William Morrow, an imprint of HarperCollins Publishers.

FIRST WILLIAM MORROW PAPERBACK EDITION PUBLISHED IN 2013.

Designed by Diahann Sturge

Library of Congress Cataloging-in-Publication Data has been applied for.

ISBN 978-0-06-200722-3

13 14 15 16 17   OV/RRD   10 9 8 7 6 5 4 3 2 1

dedicated, with love...

to the rockers who turn on the
music one second after they
turn on the lights...

. and .

to my beloved parents,
  Coco + Arie Kopelman
who never made me
turn it down.

 JK

ACKNOWLEDGMENTS

NOT IN A KATHY BATESIAN WAY, I WANT TO THANK MY OWN rock idol, Trent Reznor. I'm not a psycho rabbit-boiling fan, but I can say that Nine Inch Nails has been one of the most consistent sound tracks to my life since I was sixteen and this book wouldn't have been written without his songs.

As for my reality: This novel is dedicated to all the people below, the family and friends who are the cheerleaders that help my lazy ass limp to the computer even when I don't feel like writing.

May Chen, my goddess of an editor, you are the dream boss and I'm sofa king lucky to've found you. Jenn Joel, übergent and sage advisor—worship. And to all the Harper-Collins and ICM posse, massive thanks for everything: Liate Stehlik, Seale Ballinger, Amanda Bergeron, Shelly Perron, Clay Ezell, John Kotik, and Josie Freedman. And to Steven Beer and Mary Miles of Greenberg Traurig.

Merci à la prochaine Ellen Von Unwerth, fashion photographer Pamela Berkovic, who made me look *way* better than I am.

To my incredible friends and supporters who helped make my little wacky labor of love *Sometimes I Feel Like a Nut* a bestseller: Tara Lipton, Alexis Mintz, Trip Cullman, P.J. Tiberio, the lovely Carol Bell and Barbara Martin, Julia Van Nice, Carrie Karasyov, Vern Lochan, Jordana Sackel, all the Heinzes, Konstantin Grab, Ellen Turchyn, Marisa Fox and Michael Bevilacqua, Dan Allen, Laura Tanny, Michael Kovner and Jean de Montaillou, Kelley Ford Owen, Jennifer Linardos, Abby Gordon, Lynn Biase, Mandy Brooks, Andrew Saffir and Daniel Benedict, Richard Sinnott, Lizzie Tisch, and Jeanne Polydoris. And to the chères Vanessa Eastman, Lauren Duff, Jeannie Stern, Dana Jones, and Dr. Lisa Turvey, for being my first reader, as always.

To all the Kargmans and Kopelmans, so many thanks and many xoxoxos, especially to my parents, Arie and Coco, and to my brother, Will, and the amazing Drew. I love you so. And to Harry and the Karglings—thank you for allowing my fantasy and giving me my roots.

PROLOGUE

I like nonsense, it wakes up the brain cells.
Fantasy is a necessary ingredient in living.
—Dr. Seuss

I'VE NEVER DONE HEROIN, BUT IN THAT MOMENT OF RUN-
ning to see him again, I felt like a junkie sprinting to meet
her dealer, waiting to cook up the smack in the spoon, tie
the tourniquet on my arm, fill the needle slowly, close my
eyes softly, and surrender my soul to utter bliss once more.
I've never craved anything in my life as much as him. Not
schlong per se, but heart; his arms around me, my head on
his chest again, safe. I was fiending, pacing, agasp. I needed
him in the marrow of my bones. And I prayed I could get my
fix once more. I had the perfect life and it turned course so
drastically, as if overnight. I ached inside. But I guess they
call it growing pains for a reason.

CHAPTER 1

PROLOGUE

LUCKY FOR ME, OFFICES DON'T COME COOLER. BADASS Games had hatched in a humongous industrial former storage building near the water in Dumbo, Brooklyn, when its only product was the blockbuster Pimps N' Ho's, Volume I. A video game junkie since childhood, I was teased mercilessly by my sister Kira for years until she realized I possessed a skill set that made the boys want to hang with us. We always had the latest state-of-the-art consoles, and our house was the go-to hangout place after school for all our friends, who enjoyed procrastinating, scarfing down my famous nachos—a daily trashtastic concoction of chips, cheese, and mushrooms—and the sweet-defeat of being trampled by me in game after game of Nintendo.

HAZEL, YOU ARE THE WINNER!

Kira thought it was a tad odd, this addiction of mine, and would often be upstairs with her blond ponytail friends talking about the upcoming dance or a shopping trip to the mall, while I was with joystick and wide eyes down in the rec room, discovering secret magic coins, slaying dragons, and ascending level after level. When my parents balked, I used every young gamer's weary echoed refrain "it's really good for hand-eye coordination!"

When I rocked Super Mario Bros. and saved the princess all by my lonesome, I was, in a way, signifying to myself that I didn't need a guy to come rescue me from an ivy-wrapped stone tower. I'd fucking save my own ass, thank you very much. My video games accompanied me to college, then to my shared rental with Kira on the Lower East Side after school, and soon after my move, I gave an emotional middle finger to all the people who thought my dorkissssima obsession was not only not feminine but also actively weird; I landed a killer job working for Noah Tannenbaum, a pioneer in the industry. I turned my basement fixation into a career.

"You're a cutie pie," Noah had said, looking me over in his renowned lothario's gaze. I was wearing my uniform of black leggings and a black T-shirt, probably a vintage concert collectible from The Void, I can't recall.

"Uh, thanks," I replied sheepishly, feeling his eyes float down from my bobbed dyed-black hair down past my wrists full of chunky bracelets south to my leather ankle boots.

"You're a real gamer?" he asked.

Without even answering, I walked to the mega setup across from the massive couch in his office and fired up Buck Hunter. I picked up the simulation .22 shotgun worthy of the woods of Alabama. Every Bambi I spied was toast within minutes, and I'd beaten his high score.

"Holy shit!" he exclaimed. We talked shop for an hour over a catered lunch and I was hired by the end of the day to help him roll out. Through my twenties my responsibilities grew and by twenty-nine I was the global head of marketing and PR. Work was my life, pretty much. Guys came and went, but Badass was my anchor.

I had always been fiercely independent. While I had some very intense passionate long-term romances—a gorgeous swimmer in college, a sexy artist in Williamsburg—it wasn't until I met Wylie that I had that cozy feeling. We fit. Physically, mentally, everything. I don't mean that like penis-and-vagina-style, I mean our bodies somehow molded together like I was designed to nestle into his exact form. I was home.

I was at a snoozeville boringass Christmas party of Kira's best friend, Meg. Her husband was some banker guy, and I felt so out of place in their deluxe duplex on Park Avenue. After small talk with several decked-out guests that basically just consisted of me nodding, I darted off to the kitchen to steal hors d'oeuvres hot out of the oven and hang with the hot gay cater waiters, who were always more interesting than the crowds they served. One was an actor, another a songwriter. I was leaning on the marble island in the middle of the huge cooking area, when I noticed the gorgeous chef quietly adding chives to the top of his artfully made mini truffle quesadillas.

"You don't mind if I hide back here eating all your delicious food, do you?" I asked.

"No, no, not at all," he replied. "Here, try these—"

He leaned in and offered me the perfectly adorned round mushroom explosion.

It was love at first bite.

Normally peeps say that about vampires, but for me, it was my darling chef.

"Oh my god, this is fucking ambrosia!" I squealed, mouth still full.

I never was formally diagnosed, but I always thought I might have Tourette's. I have zero edit button, and while I don't spontaneously blurt out "cocksucking motherfucker" in supermarkets or anything like that, I definitely let my emotions hold the reins of my mouth, rather than my brain.

"Sorry." I shrugged sheepishly. "That was just really yummy." I blushed.

"Don't apologize." Wylie leaned in, his big brown eyes smiling. "I love a girl who likes to eat."

"Oh believe me, I do," I said, stealing another before the slick black-turtleneck-clad waiter whisked out the platter. "I'm a grade-A snarfer. I'm like a bulimic but without the barfing part."

"Really? You don't look like it. You'd think a chowhound would look like Violet Beauregarde. After the blueberry transformation. You don't seem like you're getting rolled away on a dolly anytime soon."

"Well, my sister Kira says I have a fast metabolism. But supposedly that makes you age faster. Who knows. You can't win 'em all."

"Here, try this—" He spatula'd a phyllo-dough goat cheese morsel of heaven. "Careful, it's hot," he warned, smiling.

I practically orgasmed on the Mexican tile. "HOLY-FUCKINGSHIT," I said with a full mouth. "I bet you do this with all the ladies," I accused, with a raised brow.

"Nope," he said, almost wistfully. "I seem to be married to my kitchen."

He was beautiful. He was perfect. Gorgeous, kind, a world-class chef, and clearly not an assholic womanizer? *What was this guy, a fucking unicorn?*

By the end of the night I had four thousand calories and Wylie's phone number.

CHAPTER 2

*The gift of fantasy has meant more to me
than my talent for absorbing positive knowledge.*
—Albert Einstein

WE MOVED IN TOGETHER NINE MONTHS LATER.

It was good I had a live-in boyfriend because if I had been single at my office, listening to the Neanderthal rantings of the otherwise all-male staff of thirty at work, I'd be a man-hating basket case.

"So I banged this chick last night, fuckin' insane, man," John, the head of development, bragged. "Fucking huge fake tits, blond hair to her ass crack, man. She was out of her mind, but holy shit was it hot."

"So are you gonna hit that this weekend?" my (married) boss Noah asked, living vicariously.

"Nah. The head was killer but not worth the headache, if you know what I mean. I can smell crazy the way dogs can smell fear, and this betty was fuckin' certifiable."

"It's too bad you can't use their mouths and then duct tape them up afterward," chimed in Sergei, the head programmer.

"Charming," I interjected.

Great, just great. Like Courtney Love once crooned, "When they get what they want, they never want it again . . ."

Pretending I was mute, I banged away on my oversize, fabulous, state-of-the-art Mac and wore earphones much of the day as I prepped all our marketing materials. We were launching our newest edition of our biggest-selling game, Pimps N' Ho's, Volume V, and Noah was on a press-craving rampage with enormous launch parties in New York and Los Angeles. New York was cake, it was my hometown, and having been a bit of a partier in my early twenties (read: Fiona Apple times ten), now at the dusk of that decade, I was honestly over it. But I did happen to know virtually every cool space in the city and had already booked a huge studio on Twenty-sixth Street on the Hudson.

California would prove more of a challenge. Starting with one small cringe-inducing fact: I couldn't drive. Noah wanted to put a bullet in my head because every time I had to fly out there for work he had to hire me a driver. Which literally cost like five dollars to him, since he sold half of the company to the Japanese two years ago. I had been employee lucky number seven, so I had made a bunch of dough on my stock options, enough to buy our small apartment and have some left over. I was very pleased by his generosity and where I was at the company, but annoyed he still gave me shit about my lack o' skills at the wheel. I was confused by how indignant he was, teasing me mercilessly, incessantly. I mean . . . didn't guys like to be in control while the chicks did Tawny Kitaen–style straddles on the hoods of their hot Jags? I guess guys like a woman with her hand on the big stick shift, though. Either way I knew at some point I'd have to learn but kept staving off the inevitable STUDENT DRIVER–emblazoned Ford Focus.

Noah called everyone into the all-glass conference room in the middle of the ground floor. I walked down the huge metal hanging staircase to The Pod as we all called it, where we found a spread of organic sandwiches Noah had delivered fresh every day. Despite his mildly jerktastic ways, I knew I was lucky. Jobs don't come much cooler than mine. That said, I was steeped in hellacious embryonic stages for all our press blitz and upcoming events. I'd already gotten massive promised coverage in tons of magazines, plus Noah would do a whole round of television interviews. But I was stressed beyond measure by the piling notebook pages on my skull n' bones–covered Lucite clipboard and thought I'd have a nervous breakdown before I reached my thirtieth birthday dinner that weekend.

"Hazel. What's up with L.A.?" Noah asked.

"I'm going next week for a few nights. I hired a local events gal who's supposedly awesome to help me with the Rolodex and secure the details, catering, invites etc., though I found a very cool printing press in Los Feliz."

"Okay. And celebrities. I want bold facers. I want cool edgy ones, not this B-list shit. If Stephen fucking Dorff comes to one more of our fucking parties I swear to fucking Jesus H. Tittyfucking Christ on roller skates that I will machine-gun his ass the fuck out of there," steamed Noah. "Ditto for those reality bitches. I don't want one of those sorry skanks. No butter-face housewives of Buttfuck, U.S.A. Not a one. Fuck reality. This game is about fantasy, escapism, so I don't want trampy losers to pop the bubble. I want tits on sticks, I want jocks, rockers, and actors who can fucking act. No prime-time TV people. Unless they're on HBO or Showtime."

"Got it," I responded with a crisp head nod. No sleaze-balls, check. Great, that ruled out much of Los Angeles. There goes half my guest list.

"Moving on. Christopher—"

Noah sped along around the King Arthur–esque round table we shared as I took notes and looked over some of the press kit materials my group had brought in from the printers. I ran a hand through my hair and exhaled. The month ahead would be a fiery plunge into Hades. Fuck. If only I could be *Star Trek*–beamed to the other side, a few months hence. But life didn't work that way, alas, you had to wade through the muddy parts, like it or not. The only way out is through. Plus, I should try and enjoy the next few days before my youth falls off a cliff. In seventy-two hours, after all, I'd be—gulp!—in my thirties.

CHAPTER 3

Fantasy is an exercise bicycle for the mind.
It might not take you anywhere,
but it tones up the muscles that can.
Of course, I could be wrong.
—Terry Pratchett

P.J. AND WYLIE WERE TOILING AWAY IN THE KITCHEN WHILE
Kira, Steven, Tate, Gadi, Anne, Trip, Drew, and I sipped the
intoxicating pomegranate something or other.

"What is this, Peedge?" Kira asked P.J., who had master-
fully mixed the drinks.

"They're peach schnapps Bellinis plus fresh-squeezed
pomegranate juice."

"BEYOND!" I belted after a crisp refreshing sip. "Wy,
babe, did you try this?"

"Coming in a sec," he called out from behind the stove.
Whatever he was whipping up was lassoing my olfactory
sense as well—I couldn't stop inhaling.

Moments later he came out with a tray of hors d'oeuvres—

his trademark mini wild mushroom–grilled quesadillas with charred onion relish I'd sampled the night we met, crunchy chopped-fresh-vegetable dumplings with a sweet mustard sauce, and seared chicken satays wrapped with basil in lettuce leaves tied with a chive.

"Holy shit, this is fucking awesome, man," Tate said, popping another dumpling in his mouth.

"Thanks." Wylie smiled, humbly. Everyone was clearly blown away. He was truly one of the most gifted chefs I have ever had the pleasure of knowing, let alone living with and getting spoiled rotten by. And he was so sweet about it; none of this hotshot Food Network chef style of skirt chasing and scene making—Wylie was understated and subdued, his passion for food only simmering beneath the surface versus boiling over the top of the stockpot. Wylie wasn't interested in fame or fortune, hawking a line of knives with his name scribbled on the blade. He didn't want to roll out into some chain. We'd discussed his dreams, and he honestly sincerely just wanted to cook yummy food for people who appreciated it, one meal at a time. Made with loving care. He was the sweetest, kindest soul I'd ever known. I loved him so deeply and with all my heart and all my soul. I watched him in the kitchen deftly "plating" another round of tapas and turned to see my sister, champagne flute in hand, watching me watching him. Kira was constantly asking when the fuck we'd get engaged already.

"I'd like to propose a toast," Kira said ding-dinging her crystal with her wedding-ringed finger as we gathered in the living room, wood beams on the ceiling above warming the space with candlelit votives on every surface. "To my little sis, Hazel: you're officially a hag now!" Everyone laughed. "No, but in all seriousness, I am blown away by all you've accomplished. I know I gave you shit our whole child-hood for being glued to the goddamn video games, but obvi-ously you have the last laugh, kid. And even though you're a big shot professionally and now an over-the-hill thirtysome-thing, your spirit and your sass and helloooo, your bod, are forever young. I love you, sweetie!"

"CHEERS!" Trip echoed, with P.J.

"Awww," Anne said as Gadi put his arm around her.

"And to Trip and P.J. for offering their insane kitchen and beautiful apartment for this soirée," Kira continued. "I always love your dinner parties. And of course, to Wylie. We love you and your cooking and I hope you get what you want with the restaurant people this—"

"SHHHH!" I blurted as everyone looked at me. "Ki, it's not out yet."

"What?" Trip asked.

"Please tell us you're opening your own restaurant," Anne begged.

"Guys, we're not there yet okay?" I semisnapped. "You'll be the first to know," I assured them.

"It's okay, sweetheart." Wylie smiled, taking my wrist gently. He matched our friends' eager gazes in his direction. "It looks like . . . I might be getting funding from the McEl-roy brothers."

Claps and whoops ensued.

"No way! That is MAJOR," said Annie, who worked at *New York* magazine and instantly knew the legendary res-taurateurs' famed names. "Wylie, congrats!"

"Babe, it might not work out," I cautioned, heeding his own advice to zip it until leases were signed and money wired. "I thought—"

"Well, it's our friends, babe! If it doesn't work out they'll still love me, right?" he joked. "Plus I think it will turn out well. Things always work themselves out. And speaking of which, dinner is served."

We started to walk toward the dining table, beautifully lit with votives and hurricanes, and fragrant with fresh-cut peonies brought by Gadi and Anne.

"Wylie, in case you all didn't know, is the most optimistic person on the face of the earth," I pronounced.

"It's true," Kira seconded. "He thinks the glass is half full even if it's three-quarters empty."

"So?" Wylie responded, carrying out platters of gorgeous appetizers, from his grilled Caesar salad to a mouth-watering Caprese to baked clams everyone immediate tore into. "It's a good thing to be a positive person, what can I say?"

"You know, it's true, Wylie, you are, like, the happiest person I know," said Trip. "You're like a happy pill with a face on it."

"A hot face," P.J. added. "Hazel, is he like James Franco's doppelgänger or what?"

I smiled, looking at cute grinning Wylie, his hands behind his head. He *was* the happiest person on the planet. And he did look like James Franco, his brown eyes twinkling in the glass hurricane lamplight, twinkling and warm.

"What's not to be happy about?" Wylie asked. "I got the best job in the world, the best friends, and of course"—squeezing my hand and lifting it—"I got my lucky charm, here. Things can't go to pot when I got a girl like my Hazel."

Choruses of awwwwws.

"Yeah well, you are always living in la-la land," I said, sipping my drink. "It's not all bliss all the time out there, ya know. There does happen to be a whole other world out there of the suffering."

"Yeah thanks, I know that," he scoffed, amused by my plunge into the darkness of reality. "She's always the prophet of doom," he joked as Kira giggled, knowingly.

"Too many apocalyptic games at your company," Drew added.

"Babe, I'm just saying that despite all that mess out there in the cruel planet, we are all here together, with heirloom tomatoes from an Amish farmer who only comes here once a month!" Wylie said, his shiny eyes beaming. "We have the simple pleasures, and . . . I have you. You know, it's like the end of *Manhattan*. When Isaac lists the things that make life worth living. The apples and pears by Cézanne, Groucho Marx, Willie Mays . . . Hazel's face."

He leaned over and patted my cheek. My heart skipped a beat, I must admit. We were both Woody Allen fanatics, and he effortlessly and brilliantly wove in parallels often.

"Thanks, my love. I love those tomatoes and this fresh mozzarella, and all that great stuff BUT, there's also lists of catastrophic horrors!" I countered. "I mean, forget even the hideous injustices and tragedies abroad or even in our own country below the poverty line, I'm talking about right here, struggling with growing up, growing old."

"Uh, it's better than the alternative, Hazel," Tate said. "It's called birthdays or dirt nap."

"Of course it is, but . . . maybe it's the industry I'm in or maybe I'm just textbook Peter Pan syndrome or whatever, but I just can't fucking believe I'm thirty!" I lamented, dropping my head into my hands.

"It's great, trust me," Anne attested, six months into her third decade. "You totally come together as a person at thirty. I think this is your year," she added with a wink.

"What's so weird to me is that there are celebrities now,

like, accomplished award-wining celebrities who are so much younger than us," Gadi said. "It drives me nuts."

"Tell me about it," Tate said. "Especially when you feel like a perv for diggin' on them."

"Please," I scoffed. "You're a man. You're allowed to do that. It's considered way more pervy when we lust after some infant."

"Like who?" Anne asked, curious.

"No one for me," I said, shaking my head. "I mean, I don't like younger guys . . ."

"Awww, she only has eyes for Wy . . . ," Anne cooed.

". . . I like older guys," I finished my sentence.

"Why on earth?" Anne asked.

"I don't know, the boys don't know anything. I like experience."

"Fuck experience! I like a young butt," Kira blurted, clearly buzzed.

"Nice," Drew said, rolling his eyes.

"Okay so: you guys. Let's go around the table and say who our celebrity crush is," Anne moderated. "Pretend you get a free pass from your significant other and you could totally bone them."

"Okay then, Anne, you're first," Trip commanded.

Anne considered her options for a moment.

"Um . . . okay . . . Orlando Bloom."

"Barf." Trip mock-puked. "Pretty boy."

"He's hot!" Annie countered, offended.

"Honey, if you can get Orlando Bloom to bang your pregnant ass then by all means free pass from me," Gadi joked.

"Thanks, honey."

"I'd do that Cullen guy from *Twilight*," Kira said, flirtatiously twisting a lock of blond hair around her finger, as if

Robert Pattinson, whose name she knew damn well, were across the room.

"Great, hon, you'll have to knock down like one thousand seven hundred teenage girls to tap that," Drew said confidently. "Mine's Natalie Portman," he added.

"What?" Tate practically squealed. "No, no, no, that's all wrong. She's too pretty, like a painting. You don't want to fuck a painting. You want some hot piece of ass in a centerfold who will fuck your brains out. I'd take Pam Anderson in 1987. Are we allowed to do time-machine versions?"

"Oh, please," I said holding down vom. "I feel like I'm at my office."

"How 'bout you, Hazel?" P.J. asked. "Who's the older guy?"

I looked down and turned a shade of cotton-candy pink, drawing breath to admit the name of the man who had slayed me since I was seventeen. Who snipped my heart into red ribbons. The star on the movie screen of my closed eyelids. The fantasy who had permeated my every thought of sex since teenagehood.

Wylie beat me to the punch. "It's Finn Schiller. She's obsessed."

"Really?" P.J. recoiled, incredulous. "He looks as if he needs a shower."

"Wait . . . EW! Finn Schiller from that band The Void?" Anne asked, her face contorted with revulsion.

"He's not *from* the band," I corrected, defensively. "He *is* the band. He writes every note of music, each searing lyric, plays every instrument."

"I never got that; why even have a band name, why not just be Finn Schiller?" asked Tate.

"He's modest. He doesn't want to be famous, he doesn't lust for limelight. Unlike the loser pretty pussies you guys crave. It's so much more masculine to lurk in the shadows versus pose on the red carpet."

"Wait, Finn Schiller had that big hit on MTV with the really sexual violent video—" Tate wondered. "That dude seems royally fucked-up."

"NO YOU DI-IN!" I wagged my finger defensively. "Don't go knocking my audio husband," I said, winking at Wylie.

"Yeah but that was like his biggest hit, but he had so many even better, more smoldering, delicious songs than that," Kira said, knowing of what she spoke. A closet mega-fan, my sister was also madly in love with him. "He is one of the best songwriters ever. *Spin* magazine said *Shameful Ghosts* is one of the top one hundred albums of all time."

"Wait, he's the guy whose songs are all like 'I hate everybody/I'm going to bang youuuu,'" P.J. sang teasingly. "He's an angry motherfucker."

"Shut up," I mock-slapped P.J.

I put my hand over my heart. "I love him."

"He's what people call a tortured soul," Kira explained, pointing her thumb in my direction. "Florence Nightingale over here loves that shit."

"No I don't. I just am drawn to him, he's always had this power over me, like he's a six-foot magnet and my bones are coated in metal."

"Okay . . . ," Tate said, thinking I was officially a weirdo.

"All the guys you selected are total fetuses!" I said, shaking my head. "They don't have the emotion, the rage, the passion that Finn does."

"What, do you know the guy?" Drew asked.

"No. But his music is so raw, so fiercely candid I sometimes feel like I do. Plus he's turning forty, so you know he has more depth and soul than the zygotes you're naming."

"Oy vey," Trip said. "Glenn Close, stage left!"

"She is his number one fan, à la *Misery*," Kira said. "Minus the hobbling."

"Yeah, tied with *you*," I retorted. "Plus I'm a good kind of fan—devoted but with a normal happy life. It's not like I'm gonna go boil rabbits on his stove."

"Speaking of dinner, let's eat while the food is still hot. I'll bring in the lasagna. And the rabbit stew for Glenn," Wylie joked, getting up from his chair, patting my head sweetly as he walked by. He entered the kitchen, and I watched how he caringly took out the rest of the food, filling the room with an incredible mouthwatering bouquet of scents. He glanced in my direction and I smiled. I was starving. And how many girls' boyfriends can deliver a feast fit for a queen? Very few.

"Yum, that smells amaaazing, Wy," my sister gushed.

"Hey, it's not every day the love of your life turns thirty," Wylie said.

Again our gang erupted in echoes of touched cooing. I smiled. Cute. Very cute. As Wylie and P.J. filled the plates with food, I leaned back in my chair and looked around the table. The tea lights flickered, my friends, my sister, and brother-in-law laughed and sipped wine as vintage Stones played. The food was amazing, the warmth of everyone's laughter so comforting, and even though I was leaving my twenties in the Urban Outfitters dust, birthdays didn't get much better than this.

CHAPTER 4

*When a fantasy turns you on, you're obligated to God and
nature to start doing it—right away.*
—Stewart Brand

WE CLIMBED INTO BED, AND WYLIE SNUGGLED BESIDE ME IN
his white T-shirt and boxers. "I just realized something," he
said with a coy glance in his chocolate-kiss eyes.

"What's that?" I asked, noticing the glimmer that meant
he wanted to have sex.

"I'll never sleep with someone in their twenties ever
again after tonight."

I laughed. "You better not!" I faux-threatened with a
finger in his face.

"I wouldn't want to," he said, seriously, touching my
arm. "I have you. I love you so much, sweetheart. Now more
than ever. Really."

I leaned over and kissed him. Our warm mouths grew
hotter as we rolled over and he climbed on top of me.

"Babe, let me hop in the shower quickly, okay?" he asked. "Actually, why don't you come with me?"

But I'd already showered before dinner and was actually exhausted and cozy on the bed, toasty under my Bloomingdale's Number 6 level down comforter. Which is basically like a slice of lava on top of you and could fry penguins in Antarctica.

"It's okay, I'm so snuggly," I said, running my hands through his hair as his chin rested on my chest. "You hop in and you can shag me rotten after."

"Done!"

He hopped up and took his clothes off. Even though nearly three years had passed, I always drew breath a bit when I saw his perfect physique. Not too big, not scrawny, just perfect, normal. Sweet. The tall chef with a Roadrunner's metabolism. He turned to smile at me before he walked into the bathroom. I heard the shower water being turned on and the curtain move to the left as he climbed in to lather up, as per his nightly ritual. He loved night showers—he usually got home from work feeling like he'd been stewed in garlic and herbs, but to me he was always yummy spices from all over, like he had the world's fields all inside of him, a potpourri of all his recipes.

As I lay there, too tired to even leaf through a catalog, let alone my *Time Out New York* magazine, I tossed a few from my pile by my suitcase so I would have reading for the plane ride. As my eyelids grew heavier, the blazing GE lightbulb didn't feel so "soft white." The wine was definitely causing my head to throb, and I decided to haul my sleepy ass out of my toasty bed to flip off the lights and stagger back to lie down in the darkness.

Oh. My. Fucking. God.

To my utter and complete shock, as my eyes hit the ceiling, they didn't see the normal eggshell paint turned gray with nocturnal shadows. Instead, as my pupils dilated in the night, I saw above me that Wylie had taken little glow-in-the-dark stars and spelled out three little words on my ceiling.

They were: MARRY ME, HAZEL.

My heart started racing faster than a shooting star. Sweat poured from my brow as I started to pant. Oh my god. My youth really was behind me. Now I was thirty. Now I'd be married. Now everything I knew of life would change. But . . . I didn't want it to. Not yet! Oh FUCK! What was wrong with me? Didn't every girl in the world pray for a gesture like this? In luminescent constellations no less? I thought I was going to suffer a heart attack. Right then and there. What do I do? Ohmygodohmygod. I looked at the phone. Too late to call Kira. I panted.

I couldn't bear to say no.

But I wasn't prepared to say yes.

The faucet turned off. The last of the water stopped dripping. My pulse was a quasar's velocity. I heard the curtain pushed back open as the towel dried my beloved's skin. But by the time he turned the door handle open, he found me, on my side curled up, eyes closed.

"Haze?" he asked. "Hazel? Are you asleep, sweetie?"

I said nothing, lying in fetal position, forcing myself to breathe slowly as my back gently moved in staged slumber. I even conjured a semisnore for reality's sake.

"Shoot. Okay," he said to himself, leaning next to me to kiss my allegedly slumbering forehead. "Good night, sweetie."

In the blackness of my Oscar-winning dead-duck per-

formance, I wondered what the fuck was wrong with me.
The dream proposal. "Cut out in little stars," Romeo and
Juliet–style.

And typical Wylie, the king of details, the guy who tied
the caviar beggars' purses with a thin bow made of chive,
even speared my heart with the punctuation he employed
in his celestial would-be proposal. In MARRY ME, HAZEL, the
comma was a comet.

CHAPTER 5

True, I talk of dreams,
Which are the children of an idle brain,
Begot of nothing but vain fantasy.
—William Shakespeare

THE NEXT MORNING I WOKE UP AND BEGAN DARTING AROUND in the darkness to get ready for my flight. I quietly gathered my toiletry kit, extra shoes, and baseball hat to shove in my mostly packed suitcase. I tiptoed, trying not to wake sleeping Wylie, and glanced at the ceiling, where his ignored proposal was still stuck, only not as brightly aglow, as early morning light was just starting to stream through the perimeter of our blackout shades. I exhaled in guilt and opened the bedroom door to sneak out and closed it behind me softly. I walked into the kitchen with my bags and peeled a fluorescent pink Post-it from the pad by the phone and scribbled on it in my trademark thin Japanese architecture pen and stuck it on the fridge door.

"Wy honey, thank you for such a beautiful bday dindin, angel. I love you xoH" it read. I looked at it against the matte silver door surface and thought of him waking up alone with the pale snot-green plastic galaxy above his sleepy head. I picked up my luggage and went downstairs.

The traffic to JFK was mercifully nonexistent as my Town Car flew down the highway, getting me to the terminal in plenty of time. The skies above looked rather threatening, but I'd signed up for texted alerts should my plane be delayed. The only problem was, I was so anal about travel, what with interminable security lines and all, that often by the time I received word of a delay I was already in Sbarro, jamming down a slice. But as this was the crack of dawn my tummy wasn't quite up for pizza, so I hoped to happen upon some sort of nonvile breakfast sandwich in my two-hour sojourn to the gate.

"Good morning, Ms. Lavery," said the chipper gal at the counter. Clickety clackety click clack went her secret counter-shrouded keyboard as I looked around at the infusion of fanny-pack-wearing travelers toting wheely luggage and neck pillows. "Anything to check this morning?"

"Uh, yeah, I have one duffel bag here," I said, plopping it on her metal scale. I wasn't a big packer. Kira literally needed four enormous Vuitton suitcases to even go for a weekend wedding within a striking distance of two hours and was always appalled by my small army tote. But I liked packing light, it was almost like a fun challenge to make all the outfits from a few separate staples. I liked my freedom though and didn't want to lug my compact but still heavy bag, so I was happy when it was tagged and taken from me.

"Now, Ms. Lavery, I see here that you have several hundred thousand miles and we really don't have a full flight this morning, so I can put you in for an upgrade, since this is a full-fare ticket," she offered.

"Cool! That would rock, thank you." I beamed. Awesome. I could arrive refreshed and chill in laid-back California.

"Check the monitor at gate fifty-one and they will set you up."

"I really appreciate that, thank you!" I smiled. Wow. I guess all my crazy travels in the last five years had accrued me some serious points.

I wandered in search of some form of huevos rancheros or an eggsdilla-type breakfast—eggies with a Mexican twist. I already had four spots in L.A. where I would bolt for the same dish each morning, but for some reason in my anticipatory craving for Angelino food my mouth was already watering for one. Even if lame-o à la Mex & The City at LaGuardia. But no such luck. There was a sports bar–type place that looked promising but wouldn't open until nine, when we would already be somewhere over Ohio. Then I saw an Au Bon Pain. Ooooh, Kira's weakness—a microwaved pain au chocolat. There was such a huge log of butter in each one that when they heated it up, the paper was positively drenched with grease, and it burned my hands just picking it up. But each bite was ambrosia and I ordered it up with a huge orange juice. I plopped at a nearby table with my tray and scoped the *Times* on my iPhone as a young couple sat at the adjacent table with their toddling daughter who was whining up a storm.

"Why don't we go to the first-class lounge?" the wife quipped, removing a leftover crust from the prior breakfaster at the Formica table. "This place is gross."

"Daddddddddddddeeeeeeeeeee! I hungwee!"

"Honey, let's just get Allegra fed and then we can go," he said, ripping off a piece of Krispy Kreme for the kid.

Uh-oh. First class? Shizzle. Maybe I didn't want my upgrade after all. I prayed this family was not sitting near me for six hours. I had traveled enough to know the neighboring passenger can make or break a flight. I tried to tune them out as I chowed my food and pounded my juice, leaving plenty of time for a magazine harvest at the newsstand before I cased the gate for seats near the boarding area.

I scored a seat and started flipping through one of the gossip rags when the din of the growing group of passengers bubbled to a white noise that I decided to block out via iPod. I plugged in my earphones and scrolled through the artists, landing on The Void and hitting play on an older tracked "Shadowed Veins" as I zoned out and closed my eyes. The industrial synth metal opening pitter pattered in violent but romantic swells until Finn Schiller's voice, beginning with a seductive whisper, purred in the left side of my earphones.

> *You stitched my damaged bleeding guts*
> *Choked and chained in muddy ruts,*
> *In my fractured, searing soul*
> *You try to burrow, render whole*
> *You pull upon the thinning strings*
> *Revealing little twisted things*
> *Regret is all you'll ever sow*
> *Against thick tides crash waves of woe.*
>
> *I'd rather stealth and slink astray,*
> *And live alone inside the gray*
> *Shadows in my veins*
> *Shadows in my veins*
> *You dig inside my gnarled past*
> *Wishing you could make us last*
> *Eclipsed in darkening shadows,*
> *Shadows in my veins*
> *So blink away those glassy eyes,*

I'll not again melt in your thighs
My contorted muscles ache
With every hallowed hope I break
I'm not the type who seethes to shatter
Lovesick dreams of those who matter
The trouble with my poison voice
Ink blotted out the word rejoice.
I'd rather simply peel away,
And live alone inside the gray
Shadows in my veins
Shadows in my veins
You dig inside my wounded past
Swearing to remain steadfast
Licked by menaced shadows,
Shadows in my veins

I ran my hand down my chilled arm as his words retreated from his trademark throat-rich growl back to a subdued hush, quiet but fiercely loaded with unbridled emotion. Never had a dulcet whisper screeched so loud. As always, I had goose bumps. This had happened before, countless times through countless years. In the most banal of settings, his sex-laced voice made me feel electrified, as if I were cut and pasted from a packed airport to a ship at sea, or a Corona ad, but with a cloud-kissed sky. A grisaille Zack Snyder movie. A moody tempest, which was so much cooler than clichéd sunshiney bullshit. There I sat once again, in the most asexual disgusting crossroads of Fanta-chugging humanity, feeling completely turned on.

CHAPTER 6

Abandon the search for Truth; settle for a good fantasy.
—Anonymous

IN THE HAZY GLOW OF MY IPOD, I CAME TO WHEN MY EAR-
phones were trumped by the loudspeaker calling my name.
I snapped out of my guitar-lulled dream and bolted to the
desk, where I was greeted with a new boarding pass.

"Miss Lavery, your upgrade came through and you'll be
in seat 3B this morning."

"YAY, okay, awesome, thank you so much."

Delights!

"Follow me, we're preboarding first class right now."

I took two steps toward the ticket scanner.

"Have a nice flight," the gentleman offered as I bounded
down the jetway. It was weird being the first on board.
The flight attendants were all lined up to welcome me and
seemed supersweet, if not a little saccharine.

"Hello, I'm Trixie, I'll be your first-class cabin attendant
this morning. Can I offer you some water, orange juice, or
champagne?" she asked.

"Uh, sure. I'll take an orange juice, please."

I'd already consumed a huge one, but what the hell, a little extra vitamin C might make me feel as healthy as the UVA-ray 'fornians I was about to look like a cadaver next to.

More first-class passengers streamed in, and mercifully the family with the whiner was on the opposite aisle from me. Soon enough the whole cabin was filled except for the seat next to me. Too bad the armrest didn't go up so I could make a minibed, like I did in coach when I lucked out with an empty row. General boarding had commenced, and I watched as everyone wheeled bags, looked at tickets and overhead row markers, and looked generally stressed about plopping for six hours. OJ finished, I decided to pop my earphones back on and disappear into the narcotic moans of The Void until takeoff. Even though I was very used to traveling, when I was alone I felt a bit riled until the *Say Anything* ding. Once seat belts could be unfastened it wasn't likely we'd be tossed around the cabin, so one could presumably breathe easy. But until then, I would have music to accompany my nerves through liftoff. I spied a woman across the aisle popping a pill, probably to calm her anxiety. Okay, I wasn't alone. I closed my eyes and drank in the opening chords of "Black Wings," which the shuffle function happened to happily land upon.

Black Wings

Impossible longing boils within
Unbridled wild urge to sin
To lunge and pounce upon your door
To coax and ravish you on the floor
Wish I could freeze this scorching pain
Scrub an eraser on my brain

So spread your black wings, black wings
Fly me to a different time
Where we can feast on pretty things
And never dwell upon our crime
Violet velvet drowned my thoughts,
Now rusted, fragile, frail, distraught
Spread your black wings, black wings.

Yearning grips me like a snake
Rewind the night you called mistake
My thirst has reached a fevered pitch
You teased, you preyed, you little bitch
So now I armor up with steel
The man who used to bend and kneel.
So spread your black wings, black wings
Fly me to a different life
Where I, to you alone, can sing
And never dwell upon the strife
Sepia postcards stained my thoughts,
Now rusted, fragile, frail, distraught
Fly off, black wings, black wings.

As the final staccato string plucks slowly faded, I heard rumbling next to me and opened my eyes. NOTHING in my thirty years had prepared me for the shock of whom I beheld.

My neighbor, boarded as the cabin door was closing, was the very man who had sung me through the airport: Finn Schiller. My fantasy, my icon, my rock god, in seat 3A.

CHAPTER 7

Fantasies are more than substitutes for
unpleasant reality; they are also dress rehearsals, plans.
All acts performed in the world begin in the imagination.
—Barbara Grizzuti Harrison

HOLYSHITHOLYSHITHOLYSHITHOLYSHITHOLYFUCKINGSHIT.

I felt seized by volts of stunned currents, as if all the amps from his recent North American tour were hooked up to the base of my spinal column. I sat up straight and looked down into my bag with a feigned curiosity, as if its contents held the mysteries of the universe. As I tried to control my breathing, I mimicked perps who try and beat the lie detector; playing it cool while in reality I was a pulse-pounding mess. An impromptu electrocardiogram would have revealed wild squiggles up and down, the needle vibrating as if recording a Richter scale over the delicate squares of powder blue–lined graph paper.

This can't be happening.

As he tucked his bag into the overhead compartment, I got a peripheral glance of his black leather motorcycle jacket over a light gray T-shirt and black jeans. I felt a stinging insti-sweat burn the back of my neck, knowing I was now a shade akin to fuchsia. My eyes fell on my iPhone, which was on the shared armrest, and they widened in alarm at his lyrics on the screen! Quickly, I shoved my phone in my bag, praying he hadn't already seen the image he'd commissioned from an Angelino artist, a graphic paper cutout with the words of the song written over it in a haunting calligraphy, as if rendered by a quill and inkwell.

Not only was this an artist so far beyond the realm of mortals, but he was also technologically way ahead of the curve vis-à-vis other musicians, embracing the Web and new gadgets in ways others only caught onto after the craze. He wasn't an early adopter but a pioneer, seeking young companies to keep him on the cutting edge of what his fans were up to online. He was a guerrilla marketing genius, and I had ripped many pages from his book in terms of marketing our games in outside-the-box ways. The first to sell media-rich MP3s that came with accompanying images and lyrics, his poetry was right there on my phone.

I pulled my phone out quickly and texted my sister.

KI. U R GONNE DIE. SITTING NEXT TO FINN SCHILLER.
FUCKING WIGGING.

He came back from the galley with a champagne in one hand and an orange juice in the other, and sat down next to me as I casually turned my phone off.

"Hi there," he said.

Fuck, what do I do, play it cool? Yes. "Hi."

"A little stormy out there." He gestured out the window with a jut of his Bernini-carved jaw.

"Yeah, hopefully Zeus won't chuck down too many bolts our way." Where the hell did that come from?

"God, I fucking hope not," he said, swigging his bubbly. "You headed home?"

"No, um, I live here. Just going for a few days for work. Business trip." OMG DORK! Redundant. Dumbass. I felt like when my niece couldn't pronounce *stupid* and just said "toopid . . ." I was so fucking toopid.

"Yeah? What do you do?" I saw him look me over with my charcoal T-shirt and black jeans. My gray Converse slip-ons were probably the giveaway that I didn't have a normal desk-job.

"I work for Badass Games? We make—"

"You're shitting me," he said, angling himself toward me more. "You work for Badass Games?! Are you fucking kidding me? I play all your games on a loop! I shattered my Xbox when I got Road Warriors Two. The band and I were addicts, man. I'm so pumped for Pimps N' Ho's Five."

Knock me over with a feather . . . we were on Finn Schiller's radar? Little ol' moi was, by proxy, as the Little Mermaid sang, *part of his world*? I mean, I knew countless celebs used our products, as they confessed nightly on their blogs or Letterman's couch. Part of my job was pulling reels and clippings for Noah each week with all the mentions from those whose hands and feet had been pressed into the wet cement on Hollywood Boulevard—he was such a fame-fucker he practically got hard when he learned Pamela Anderson played our games with her sons.

"Wow, that's great!" I said like a grade-A nerdling. "I'm actually flying out to work on our launch. We're having a party in L.A. the day the game drops next month."

"No shit!"

"Shit."

He smiled. "I'm Finn, by the way," he said, extending his hand.

"Yeah, I know, hi," I replied, casually, shaking his hand as I thought I would swoon and keel over and do a faceplant onto my open tray table. "I'm Hazel."

"Hazel. I dig it," ignoring that I totally knew who he was. "Like witch hazel."

"Yes, just like witch hazel," I confirmed with a note of ice in my clenched reply.

"The kids call you that when you were little?" he asked, leaning back, exploring my face as I smiled shyly.

"What do you think?" I asked rhetorically.

"Man. Kids are cruel." He shrugged. "But you certainly don't look like a witch. You look like a good witch. The kind that's beautiful," he said as I looked away, dying. "The kind of witch who made them invent the word *bewitching*."

Um . . . get me some defibrillators PRONTO. Did Finn Schiller, banger-of-models, just use the word *beautiful* relating to me? Or was it that I just wasn't a hideous green bewarted crone? Breathe, Hazel.

"Thanks." I smiled. "They actually made me check my wand in my suitcase, no more carry-on wands," I deadpanned. "You know, if it fell into the hands of Al Qaeda, there would be hell to pay."

I saw his brow crinkle a bit as the plane started to taxi down the runway. He smiled a mysterious grin as I felt the small hairs on my whole body stand on end, as if my palms were resting on a glowing glass nebula sphere with that blue light inside, like sixth-grade science class. Kira is going to die. Kira is going to frigging die.

"Ladies and gentlemen, this is Captain Lord here on the flight deck," a teenager's voice said. I looked at Finn. "We're next in line for takeoff so sit back and relax and enjoy the flight to Los Angeles."

"Is it me or does he sound prepubescent?" I asked.

"He fucking IS," my idol testified, hand-on-heart. "I got on board at the last minute and met him, the dude is twenty-fucking-four."

"How do you know?" I asked.

" 'Cause he looked like fuckin' Doogie Howser and I asked him."

Great. I glanced out Finn's window, which was now splattered by diagonal raindrops lashed by the wind before they hit the Plexiglas. The slanted drawn-out drops pelted the wing as I gulped. Here we go.

CHAPTER 8

Fantasy, abandoned by reason,
produces impossible monsters; united with it,
she is the mother of the arts and the origin of marvels.
—Francisco de Goya

THE DING CAME QUICKLY AS WE HIT CRUISING ALTITUDE
without much shaking, and I was about to exhale in relief
when the pubes-less pilot came on once more.

"Ladies and gentlemen, Captain Lord here again. It
seems the front we were trying to avoid is right in our flight
path, due west about a hundred miles. It's gonna be a bit of
a bumpy ride, so please keep your seat belts on at all times.
Thanks."

"Gee, just what I wanted to hear," I said to Finn, who was
leaning back so I could see out his window. What had been
a whiteout was now a textured thick blackening cloud with
whirls of gray and black laced in like an ethereal, mushy
marble. This did not look good.

"This does not look good," Finn said, which somehow
sent me into a panic. He was probably Executive Platinum

in mile count, and if he looked nervous, I was surely toast. Thank god I didn't have that Activia yogurt from my fridge or I'd've surely shat.

Lightning flashed as the plane bounced abruptly, causing the little girl across the cabin to shriek.

I gripped my left armrest and exhaled as the plane started surging in an up-and-down roller coaster of clouds with no tracks.

Silence filled the cabin as I noticed other passengers white knuckling the armrests or gripping spouse's hands in sheer terror. I thought of Wylie, asleep in our bed. Our safe, nonshaking, firm-on-the-floor bed. I felt a beat of guilt about his thwarted efforts but was jolted from my vision of his sweet fluffy slumbering head with a drop that had to be fifty feet. Screams worthy of Munch.

I turned to Finn, and my heart pounded even faster.

"I'm really freaked-out," I said, whitening away from my crush-blush into a fear-kissed pallor as my four servings of acidic OJ were sloshing inside me.

"Don't worry," Finn calmed me, though I could see a flash of nervousness in his blue eyes as he continued to stare out the window at the menacing mist. "It'll level out, we're in the eye of it now," he assured me.

"I don't feel so good," I confessed, grimacing as I put a hand to my rumbling tummy of citrus hell. The plane suddenly plummeted what felt like a hundred feet and SCREAMS filled the cabin and the lights flickered on and off. "Oh my god," I added, trying not to cry. My obituary would say that I died on that doomed Finn Schiller flight. Great. My blue-state self would be in ashen shards scattered over some rectangular red one.

Just then the plane dropped, and Finn grabbed my hand. He squeezed it, and I could tell it was a perfectly natural we-

are-totally-about-to-die instinct. Though we were complete strangers, we were now bound to each other as we buzzed the doorbell on the Crypt Keeper's cobwebbed lair. Here we go. Bye-bye world. Our fingers intertwined, and even with the tearing eyes that blurred my vision, his touch made me see stars.

Trying to swallow hard as the plane jostled back and forth, up and down, with my free right hand I leafed past the magazines in the seat pocket in front of me and retrieved the dreaded barf bag. I'd never used one, except when I held it open for Kira on a flight to Colorado during one of her pregnancies. But from what I could hear around me—gagging sounds of upchucked chunder—I was not alone in my gut-gripping nausea.

The next thing I knew, Finn had his hand on my rounded back, gently moving it up and down. "Just breathe," he said in his trademark whisper. I could not fucking DEAL this was too insane. I felt the bottom half of my being melt into the cheesily upholstered taupe pleather airplane chair. Never had a body been through so much at the exact same moment—a tsunami of hormones for both sex and fear. Talk about Eros and Thanatos. During college I'd written a paper on sex and death enmeshed in paintings. Now I was coloring a canvas of my own as the man who personally brewed the potent teenage tea of my sexual fantasies had his hand on me when I was just seconds from my fate.

"Oh my god, I am so sick. I—"

Horrifyingly, an unstoppable wave of chunder was unleashed by my esophageal passageway and I hurled violently into the bag. Like, full-body racking with vom. Right there, with *Spin* magazine cover boy next to me. I envisioned a *Stand by Me* chain reaction barf-o-rama where the whole plane would deliver pavement pizzas because of a whiff of my toxic taco-tossage. I suddenly recalled, as my cool fourth-grade English teacher Miss Morse pointed out, you can always remember the word *embarrassed* is spelled with two *s*'s because when you feel embarrassed it's as if your ass is hanging out. Okay, so my butt wasn't exposed but my breakfast certainly was. And just when I was dying of mortification so intense I thought Brad Pitt-as-Death-personified-in-that-horrendous-movie would pluck me then and there before crashing our plane, I felt Finn's fingers on my hair, delicately pulling it back into a ponytail, held together by his encircling hand. A hand that had held Grammy awards for chrissake.

"I'm so sorry," I managed to squeak out between pants of agony. "This is so gross I'm so horrified."

"Shhhh," he soothed me, rubbing my back as it racked with a new wellspring of Au Bon Vomit. "It's okay, little witch. Get it all out."

The plane took another massive plummet as voices from all thirty-seven rows let out screams and cries, with a rising tide of vocal whimpers filling the space.

"Ladies and gentlemen, Captain Lord here again—"

"I love it, his name is synonymous with God," Finn said.

"Looks like we are almost through the worst of it, another few minutes to go, hang in there. I must say, this is the worst turbulence I've seen in my career."

How comforting! Thanks, Cap'n.

I shot Finn a look. "Yeah, his five-minute-long career."

"Stay put, I'm gonna get you some water."

"It's okay, really, they're gonna freak if you stand up—"

He stood up. He gripped the tops of the seats and planted his legs as he stepped up the aisle of the plane. Trixie flight attendant was strapped into her gimp seat and began to shout at him. "SIR! SIT DOWN NOW!" she yelled, prompting every passenger within earshot to crane their necks.

"She needs water. She's really sick," he said.

Lancelot, thou art not armor-clad but in a steel-hued T-shirt. My stomach was in shambles as was my arrow-speared heart.

"I SAID SIT DOWN!" she bellowed. "SIDDOWN!" Clearly the blond bouffanted Carrie Underwood–listening Georgia peach had no clue who the fuck she was talking to.

Ignoring her, Finn reached into the galley and grabbed a bottle of Poland Spring and made his way back to row three, despite country-fair-style Pirate Ship rocking. He sat next to me, unscrewing the cap, and handed me the bottle. It was such relief to get the putrid taste from my mouth. Slowly, the pitch of the plane's torturous free-fall descents decreased. I breathed as if breaking through the finish line of a marathon. Through the Alps.

"It's over now," he said, taking the bottle from my shaking hand and putting the top on. He continued with his puke-ponytail to gather the hair from my quivering lips.

"It's okay. Looks like we made it."

CHAPTER 9

In my sex fantasy, nobody ever loves me for my mind.
—Nora Ephron

AFTER A FEW MINUTES OF STEADYING MY BREATH AND DE-
compressing, I exhaled a slow, long sigh and met Finn's ice
blue eyes.

"Oh my god, thank you so much, you're an angel."

"Nah, that I ain't. I lost my halo a looooong time ago. I've
had a lifetime of being less-than-good, and it's disappeared
and irreplaceable, I'm afraid. I filled out all the necessary
paperwork and everything and they said it was gone for
good."

"I don't believe that. You're not so bad," I said with a
knowing smirk.

"How do you know?" he asked with a sexily arched
brow. As he leaned in, his motorcycle jacket made that delicious sound of grinding leather. I thought I would pass out.

"I just know. From the music. You know, yes, there is
this incredibly passionate violent side, but it's infused with
romanticism as well, the lyrics, the aesthetic of the videos. I

have always loved things that are both romantic and violent at the same time," I said, shrugging my shoulders. "I guess to me your albums pretty much embody that idea."

He sat, staring at me. Then the grinding leather again as he leaned back. He looked at me silently, as if his interest were suddenly piqued by something I said.

"What?" I asked.

"Hazel."

"Yes?"

"What's your last name?"

"Lavery."

"How do you know so much, Miss Hazel Lavery?"

"I don't." I shrugged. "I mean, I don't know. I just know that when I was told under penalty of being Tasered upon arrival and shoved into Airport Jail by Trixie the once-perky flight attendant if I so much as attempted to hit the lavatory and was compelled to then vomit in front of a world-renowned rock star, well, I just know that you were . . . incredibly sweet about it all. I'm really grateful. I was bent over chundering and not only did you not freak, you helped me. I'm sure most girls around you are bending down for other reasons," I said with a slight diss to his fellatrix groupies.

He burst out laughing.

"You have zero edit button and I fuckin' dig it." He smiled wickedly.

We talked for the next few hours—skipping lunch and movies, just gabbing. About everything. EVERYTHING: childhood, music, movies, fears, foods. There was something so surreal yet also so comfortable and normal about it. There were some things I already knew (where he grew up, that he was orphaned at nine by a tragic car accident and raised by his great-aunt) and some unexpected revelations ("I'm a Tim Burton fanatic," "I have an egg and cheese on toast for breakfast three hundred sixty-five days a year"), but the key was seeing the glint in his eyes as he told me aspects of his life and travels that one simply can't pick up in The *Rolling Stone* Interview.

"I used to live in Chicago," he said. (Yeah, I know—he famously bought an old funeral home and made a studio downstairs where they had drained the bodies. Good times.) "That was the nadir of my life. I mean, aside from when my parents died, but I was into some dark shit there."

"What, like drugs?" I probed.

"Like drugs, yeah, bad people, bad stuff."

I took that to mean whores but wasn't quite sure.

"I'm picturing full-raging bacchanalia of wine, women, and song, slash sadistic orgies," I said.

He smiled, and I detected a note of embarrassment. Bingo. "You're not too far off."

The good thing about my Wylie is that I knew exactly where he'd been. He'd literally had enough sex partners to count on one hand, and this one clearly had enough notches on his headboard to render the whole bed sawdust.

"Are we talking like full *Pulp Fiction* leather gimp outfit with zipper mouth?" I asked while casually sipping water.

"No, actually. People always think I'm some masochist because of my videos, but that's all my director's vision. Romanek is amazing. The music has a tortured edge, I'll admit. But that doesn't mean I want to be tortured. Physically."

"Oh, good. You don't want to end up like Michael Hutchence, dangling from a noose with your ween out. You can have a million *Billboard* hits but then people will just talk about how you croaked with your schwantz at large."

"I've actually never tried autoerotic asphyxiation," he confessed. "I don't think it's for me."

"Really?!" I hammed it up. "No strangling mid-'gasm!

Boo! You big bore. What kind of fucking rock star are you?"

"Don't worry, I'm not that innocent."

"Okay, Britney."

He smiled and looked at me. "I'm serious. I may be too old to plunge on the dark side for too long like I used to, but I . . . I'm still no angel, let's put it that way."

"You know what I think?" I asked.

"What's that."

"You know on the SATs that comparisons section? Dog is to Puppy as Cat is to Kitten?" Wait, why the fuck did I mention SATs? It's not like he took them or anything. Right?

"Sure."

Weird, as I couldn't picture him filling in those torturous bubbles.

"They do those on Conan," he added. Ah-ha.

"Okay," I said. "Well, I think that the Tin Man is to a heart as you are to a halo."

"Oh yeah?" he scoffed.

"Yeah. It was there all along. You think it's so MIA, but maybe you just didn't see it, with your whole badass tough cookie schtick. But I say it's there."

His eyes flashed as he looked down at his lap.

"Interesting," he said to me curiously. "You're a perceptive girl."

I shrugged, embarrassed. But also as if to say, *hellz, yeah.*

Not to be cocky, I mean, I wasn't better than anyone, and I certainly was outdone in smarts and looks by a myriad of women, but not the women he probably hung with. In fact I suspected I was the first non-G-string wearer in his presence in years. I may not be nearly as smokin' as them, but I most certainly was with-it, probably more than most girls he spent time beside. Or on.

"I'm special, special, so special, special!" I Chrissie

Hynde-ed, mocking my props from my i◼︎
accept gracefully.

"You are." He laughed.

"At least there's no one I know who◼︎
a rock star and then talk to him. Most◼︎
tend there's something really interesting about those cloud
formations and keep their neck permanently turned to the
window until disembarking before flopping dead of humili-
ation on the baggage carousel. Just you wait, I'll be in a
chalk outline going around and around next to the Rolla-
board explosion."

"You're definitely different," he mused. "Why do you
think?"

I felt myself perspire a bit.

"I don't know. Planes are weird. It's like this passing
intersection of people. You climb on this machine together
and float up above the earth, above your real life and the
people that make it what it is," I said. "We're in this metal
pod and so I guess I leave all my issues, including intimi-
dation by major celebs, on the ground. I never would have
started talking to you at a party or in the stool next to me at
a bar, I guess. Basically my vomit broke the ice."

He held up his juice to my water bottle.

"To your vomit."

I laughed and clinked plastic. "And to your breaking
FAA laws by procuring water to rinse said vomit."

"Where did you come from?" he asked, almost rhetorically, like perhaps I hailed from Mars.

"Sixty-first Street."

He ran a hand through his hair.

"Ladies and gentlemen, this is Captain Lord from the
flight deck and it looks like we are getting clearance to land,
and we should be on the ground in about fifteen minutes. In

years in the cockpit, I must say this was the worst
her I've endured, and the whole crew and I are very
ateful for your patience and bravery during that turbulence. We truly appreciate it. Flight attendants please pre-
pare for landing."

As we put our seatbacks up, we were reminded the contents of the overheads may have shifted during takeoff and
landing . . . and, ahem, *during* the flight, given the torna-
dolike salad tossing in which we felt about as weighty as
a crouton. Finn continued to look my way as I zipped my
belongings up and braced for landing, which was smooth in
comparison to our death-grazing free fall over John Cougar
Mellencamp–land.

"We did it," Finn said, smiling.

"Would it be bizarre if I kissed the floor at LAX?"

"The tarmac might be cleaner." He smiled.

"Wouldn't it be funny if I survived this and then died on
the freeway?"

"God forbid!" he said, alarmed.

"I thought you sang 'God Is Dead'?"

"How the fuck do I know? I make this shit up as I go
along." He laughed. "Just don't joke about biting it, Hazel
Lavery. The world needs you to stick around a while
longer, K?"

"Okay," I said, getting up to begin filing to the plane's
exit. "Well, thanks again. I really think you are the reason I
survived and didn't have a complete coronary." Little did he
know his presence also spiked my blood pressure, but that
was beside the point.

"Nonsense, Lioness. You had the courage all along."

Touché.

Fuck, he was so gorgeous I wanted to touché him. As I
felt my heart and libido tug, I shook my head like a cartoon

trying to shake that water mirage in the desert. *Boyfriend, boyfriend, boyfriend. Amazing one whom you adore.*

"How're you feeling now?" he asked, putting his hand on my shoulder.

"Uh, so-so." Lies. I was electrified. There must've been a hand-shaped sunburn mark where his paw touched.

"Feel better." He smiled. "Here we go."

Trixie opened the cabin door, and as first classers we were off before the hordes of socks- and sandal-wearing plebeians, i.e., me usually. We walked off the jetway, me right behind him. Finn was pulling a small suitcase on wheels, and I just had my tote, as my duffel was checked through. As I saw him head to the departures door, where he obviously had someone waiting for him, circumventing the conveyor belt–seeking drones, he quickly turned around to look for me.

"I'm headed this way," he said. "Bye, Hazel,"

"Bye! Sorry we didn't meet under less vomitorious circumstances."

"No problem, really."

And that was that.

I exhaled, and seven hours of stress, emotion, and shock wheezed their way through my weary lungs. I reached into my pocket to turn on my cell and found not one not two but seven texts from Kira freaking about Finn, and one from Wylie asking me to text him when I landed and sending me xoxos. I quickly texted him back I was safe 'n' sound on terra firma in California and then clicked to dial Kira.

"Holy shit," she answered, clearly seeing my digits on caller ID. "TALK!"

"I know. Ki, I'm dying. DYING! We literally gabbed for five hours. I barfed in front of him, he patted my back and moved my hair—"

"Wait, WHAT?! You puked?"

"It was the worst flight in the pilot's history and every-one was screaming and chundering. It was the apocalypse. You don't understand, he—"

"Hazel!" I heard yelled from behind me. I turned around.

It was HIM, calling me from across the baggage claim carousel.

"Oh my god, is that him?" Kira gasped on the phone. "Holy fucking fuck—"

"I'll call you back." I hung up the phone and swiveled, as if on air.

"Hi," I said, walking over. The carousel beeped, alerting us it was going to start barfing out our bags. Finn met me halfway.

"Hazel, I have a car here and some lunch. You've had a long morning. Why don't you let me take you to your hotel."

"Um . . ."

"Just say yes."

"Yes . . ." I looked at the belt, not wanting to keep a huge fucking world-renowned rock star waiting. "Oh, here's my bag!" Great. "Benefits of a first-class ticket."

Without a word, a tall guy in jeans and a white tee, cov-ered in tattoos, reached over me and grabbed my fabulous vintage army duffel. To me it was chicer than any logo or zippered bells and whistles. The faded gray LAVERY was the only name I needed.

"It was my grandfather's," I said to Finn.

"It's amazing." He nodded. "This is Sly. Sly, Hazel."

"Hey," he replied. He shook my hand with his left hand as he slung my enormous bag over his shoulder as if it were stuffed with feathers. He walked ahead of us.

"The car's out this way." Finn smiled as I looked up at him. "Let's go."

CHAPTER 10

I think we dream so we don't have to be apart so long.
If we're in each other's dreams,
we can be together all the time.
—Calvin and Hobbes

ASIDE FROM OUR FLIGHT, THERE IS LITTLE THAT IS MORE NAU-
seating than the hyperbola-shaped rocky waters of guilt. I
was lilting over each booming crest as if I might capsize,
but the elation of my ride with Finn got me past the fact that
I was emotionally cheating on Wylie by suppressing every
desire to dive across the armrest and rape Finn like those
shameless midwestern teens shrieking for the Jonas Brothers to deflower them. Okay . . . this was normal. Healthy,
even? Maybe? After all it was my fantasy come to life.
And hey, it was all good fun, a pity ride for the poor pukey
beeyotch he'd bonded with on the flight, and I'd never see
him again, anyway.

"So, Hazel, I want to see you again," he said. "Give me
your number, and come to one of my shows in New York
sometime."

I once again felt jolted. As if my veins had been stripped and replaced by Con Edison, each body wire ablaze. The guilt that coursed through me now was accompanied by the jittery buzz of acute longing. I couldn't stop looking at Finn. Okay, Hazel, play it cool.

"All right, here we go," said Sly, pulling into the W Hollywood.

"I'd love that, awesome."

Fuck! Awesome! Ugh was I in the eighth grade? In 1985?

"You are," he said, leaning in to hug me. "I'll let you know when I'm back."

NO WAY! He passed over his phone and I punched in my digits, which might as well have been all sevens. I just felt that lucky.

"Okay, great, here you go!" I didn't want to get out of the car. But Sly opened my door and was handing my bag to the porter. "Bye, Finn." I smiled warmly. "Thank you so much."

"My pleasure. Bye, Hazel."

He closed the door, and they pulled away as I entered the hotel and floated to the front desk as if on roller skates. I was Hermès. Not the handbag people, the original wing-footed messenger, flying high. I got my electronic keycard and with a chill up my spine, entered the elevator feeling like the gliding angels in the Nutcracker ballet, and cruised up to the top floor to my suite. Normally I would methodically unpack so that all my clothes "don't wind up looking like accordions," as Kira would say. But I ignored my big sister's voice and left the suitcase by the door and simply lay down in bed. I took my hand and gently stroked my arm with my fingertips, feeling the goosebumps. I felt so alive I could burst. In my handbag across the room I could hear my phone vibrating. Wylie. I couldn't move. I wanted to revel. Since Wylie was my best pal, I was dying to download and

recount my morning, but on the flip side the lover side knew
it would be callous to wax rhapsodic over another man. But
what could I do? Finn was . . . magical. Larger than life. Of
course I adored Wy, but he was, ya know, my sweet guy, my
dear heart, my roomie!

If only Finn were just sexy, but rock-stupid, I could let my
fleeting thoughts of him roll away with the tides. But he was
no testosteroned himbo who happened to have a way with
plucking guitar strings and my interest.

He was brilliant. In a way I knew that already, thanks
to his heart-piercing lyrics, but often artists have words at-
tributed to them but that are actually rattled off by some
closeted paid-off ghost writer. But now I was absosmurfly
certain that the shadows really did course through his veins
and not those of some work-for-hire faux poet. Our dialogue
on that fateful flight was so intense as we did a hand-holding
tango, with Death periodically cutting in for a twirl. It was
as if we had pressed the fast-forward button on this insti-
friendship, careening through the tumult and whizzing
past normal pacing of two strangers chatting. Something
happens in the midst of potential catastrophes, where the
person beside you, if like-minded, becomes so fused to you
that there is this illusion that they are the closest person to
you in the universe, because they were in that trench beside
you. Maybe that's why army buddies are so close, or why
Keanu and Sandra smooched in *Speed*.

Okay, whoa Nelly. I had to calm down. I exhaled visions
of clutching Finn Schiller's hand and calmly dialed Wylie.

"Babe! Yay, I was so glad when you landed safe," he
said. "How is it?"

"Wy, you have no idea how lucky I feel to have my pads
on the ground."

Wylie always called my big feet "pads" and said he loved

cooking while hearing me "padding around the apartment straightening up."

"Why? Bumpy ride."

"To say the least."

I regaled him with my escapade, toning down the Finn obsession part.

"No way!" Wylie marveled. "We were JUST talking about him! How fucking nuts is that?"

"Nuts."

"That's awesome, babe."

"Barfing on idol is not so awesome, Doodlesby Mc-Clintock." (Another nickname. We had many.)

"You'll laugh about it one day," he suggested.

I felt slightly annoyed that he didn't quite grasp that, no, I wouldn't *laugh*.

"Yeah, well, doubtful, babe. It was gnarlissssimi."

"I'm sure he's seen way worse than that, honey."

I changed the subject and asked about restaurant meetings. Things were moving along swimmingly. He was filling me in on all the details when I looked at my watch. There was bidniss at hand. I needed to go and meet with the event planner and figure out the logistics of our launch.

"Babe, I'm so sorry to interrupt but I have to get up and pull my ass together."

"Okay, babe! Talk to you later."

"Bye, Wy—"

"Hey, Haze?" he asked.

"Yeah?"

"You said you'd call me more this trip, right?" he reminded. He'd said I barely checked in the last time I'd gone away and it bummed him out.

"Yes, I will," I promised. "Love you."

"Love you so."

I hauled my ass off the bed, got dressed, and went to splash some water on my face. When I closed my eyes, I pictured Finn's ice blue eyes. When I patted my cheeks dry, I caught sight of myself; I looked flushed and aglow. Oh boy. The thirty-year-old schoolgirl, how ridiculous.

Even more insane was that at my untender age I could not drive. Never learned. Never needed to. I always knew I wanted to go to school in New York where everyone walked everywhere. Some of my friends did share houses in the Hamptons (or as I call them, Cramptons, due to SUV traffic that induces suicidal thoughts) or "the islands" off Massachusetts, but the Lilly Pulitzer and whale pants explosion tended to make me itch more than the mosquitoes that devoured my flesh. I was sure, to the buzzing menaces, that I tasted something like warmed brioche bread pudding made by my Wylie. Better to stay in the city. Hence, no wheels.

So there I was, in the driving capital of the world, with my sunscreen, my shades, and my two feet. I started walking from my hotel, in search of a coffee shop, and then I would text Clarissa, the party guru, to come pick me up as I nursed espresso to further jolt my jittery blood. I took a table on the street, packed in among the countless other shade-wearing caffeine addicts, and texted her my location. As I pounded my iced beverage, I wondered who the eff all these people were and why they were just hangin' in the middle of the day with no job to go to. They couldn't, like, all be actors or screenwriters, right? Did they have family dough? Did they work at night? Sure there were areas of New York packed as well, but the city has so many tourists and it's not like there was one industry everyone was all competing to break into. Surreal.

Just as I was going to get a second cup, I jumped. My

phone vibrated once. A text message. Clarissa must be pulling up. I reached into my pocket and retrieved my new iPhone. But it wasn't her. It was another 310 number.

"Hi there. How's the tummy?" It was Finn.

As the youth of America says, "OMFG." Shaking, I hit forward to Kira and added "HLY SHT, FS TXT!" and hit send. I wasn't sure how to respond to him so I wrote "hola! Pas de vom, thank god."

Like a desperate acne'd teen, I stared at my phone on the table. Moments later, it shimmied in zapped communication. "Great! Dinner tonight?" My breath quickened as sweat started to form on my brow. Suddenly, the phone rang. Clarissa.

"Hi, doll! Pulling up now, hon!"

"Okay, I'm walking to the curb."

I quickly wrote back "sure!" and hit send, instantly regretting the exclamation point. How queer. What the fuck was I thinking? Clarissa's white BMW slowed next to me, and I hopped in, looking like the Angel of Death next to her Kira-esque blond self. I looked her over. She was definitely TOAST—Tits On A Stick, and her French manicured paws and feeties made her look part porn star part Texan cheerleading virgin.

"Girl, you need some sun, love!" she said, glancing at me through her oversize Nicole-Richie-during-Rachel-Zoe-era shades.

"Yeah, I kinda boil myself in sunscreen, actually. Instant lobster. I'm Irish and super fair."

"Oh s'all right honey, I can take you to Hollywood Tans, where Jennifer Aniston and everyone goes! You just strip down and put these goggley things on and they hose you down in brown!"

Sounds attractive. I'd rather be Smurf-blue than cheesily

airbrushed orange-beige, but I changed the subject while praying for the phone to vibrate again as my stomach did not just somersaults but full-on triple back handspring round-offs worthy of the Romanians.

"First I'm gonna take you downtown. There are two huge event spaces I use there that rock—industrial, loftlike, very New York, very airplane hangar chic. Let's see what you think."

The first was great but not heart attack–inducing. She tried to explain that at night the vista was even more amazing, but it felt like I'd seen it before. The second was quite impressive, with huge cavernous ceilings and pipes running over the ceiling but again, not mind-blowing, and I wanted my boss's eyes to explode from the sockets.

"Let's keep going," I said, sighing to a somewhat disappointed Clarissa. "I like this area though, let's try and stick downtown. It feels more in sync with the style of the game, and we've done the whole beach thing, I like the gritty city vibe of this part better."

As we were walking out, my phone rang. Vomit times ten. Finn! Holyshitholyshitholyshit.

"Hello?" I said, trying to quell the quake in my voice. My nerves could have registered on the Richter scale they were so tremor filled.

"Hazel. It's Finn."

"Hi!" I said, sounding like a fucking teen. "Um, so psyched for dinner, that's great." Ugh, *psyched*?! Did I say teen? I meant 'tween.

"Yeah, I'll pick you up at your hotel at nine. Is that good?"

"Sure, perfect."

"Do you need a minute?" Clarissa interjected.

As I nodded no, Finn said, "Oh sorry, Hazel, are you in a meeting?"

"No, uh, I'm with an event planner, looking at spaces for the party downtown."

"Yeah? God, you should use my candy factory."

"Your factory? What are you, Willy Wonka?"

"No, no, I bought this old factory and warehouse. It was an investment I guess, I got it fifteen years ago thinking one day I'd turn it into condos or something when I hang it up with the music."

What? My first thought was YOU CANT HANG IT UP! But then my job kicked in and I asked about the space, if it really was available to rent for a night.

"Rent?" He laughed. "It's Badass Games, just take it. I'd be stoked. Just let me bring a few pals, and we'll be square."

"I'm sorry, please do not tease me like this," I begged of him, looking wide-eyed at Clarissa. "Are you serious?"

"Totally. We'll stop by tonight, my manager has the keys, I'll grab them this afternoon and we can go after dinner. It's enormous and really raw with sick views. It's actually perfect for this game."

"Amazing! Oh my god, thank you so much, it sounds incredible." If he were any other person I would have instinctively added "you're such a rock star!" EXCEPT THAT HE FUCKING *WAS* A ROCK STAR.

"Okay. See you later, Witch Hazel."

I hung up feeling like a team of ER doctors just yelled "clear!" and defibrillated my chest.

"It seems we might have a potential space," I told Clarissa, in a controlled pant. "I think we may've struck party gold."

CHAPTER 11

*If one is lucky, a solitary fantasy can
totally transform one million realities.*
—Maya Angelou

CLARISSA AND I STOPPED AT HER OFFICES, BRAND LINK COM-
munications, so I could meet the girls who worked for her
(all gorgeous, manicured, and va-va-voom), and while she
hopped on a call with a fashion client, I stole a moment to
call my sister.

"I fucking cannot believe you are having dinner with
Finn Schiller."

"Kira, what do I do?"

"What do you mean, go get decked out and look your
fiercest!"

"I have a boyfriend."

Kira didn't say anything.

"Your silence is speaking volumes."

"You did get a free pass, Hazel . . . ," she teased. "At Trip
and PJ's. I heard it with my own ears."

"That was a drunken parlor game, I would never!" I protested. The second I said it I knew it was a lie. "Okay, I admit it. I can't stop thinking about it. I've been obsessed with him my entire adult life!"

"I know," she said, as if trying to help me hatch a plan. "I mean, you know I love Wylie . . . Her voice trailed off. "BUT THIS IS FINN SCHILLER!"

"Thanks, I know," I said, suppressing annoyance that my older sis wasn't doling out the magical advice she has always had at the ready.

"Okay, maybe just casually slip in something about Wylie tonight—" she offered.

"No! That's so presumptuous!" I protested. "Kira, he doesn't see me like that. We might even work together on this event!"

"Really?"

"Yeah! He has this space and he loves my company and he wants to help. I mean he so would never think of me as anything other than a pal. He has bejugged Hefner girls throwing their tanned boobies in his face! I'm pale and raven-haired and tomboyish. He wants hemlines that show your pubes, not black jeans."

"You don't know what he wants, first of all. And secondly, it's just a matter of fact, you live with Wylie, I mean you should mention that, I think."

"Okay, yeah, you're right . . ." I nodded to myself. Then I snapped out of my foolish worry. "But really it's so psycho presumptuous to think Finn Schiller would even care!"

I saw Clarissa walk up to the glass door and motion for me to come. "Anyway, I gotta go, I have back-to-back meetings until tonight."

"Please tell me you're primping a little. None of this casual Bella Swan rocker girl bullshit. Femme it up. Just a little. Please."

"Stop!" I said. "I have to go!"

"Report ASAP or sisterhood over."

"Bye, Kira!"

Ugh. I looked in the mirror in Clarissa's office as I gathered my things. I had a serious boyfriend. He was my best friend. But . . . I was dining avec the person who intrigued me most. Maybe a little effort wouldn't hurt?

CHAPTER 12

Dear love, for nothing less than thee
Would I have broke this happy dream,
*   It was a theme*
For reason, much too strong for fantasy,
Therefore thou waked'st me wisely; yet
My dream thou brok'st not, but continued'st it.
        —John Donne

CUE THE ROY ORBISON MUSIC! JUST KIDDING. NO *PRETTY Woman* primp montage for me—yet. I had to see how my meetings went. But I was a working girl—not in the Hollywood Boulevard kind of way (I'd probably score all of twenty-five bucks, if that), and I had shit to do.

First was the security firm. Four huge black guys explained how they would work the valet and press areas plus red carpet and "step and repeat"—the annoying but necessary billboard with our logo behind the velvet ropes where the celebs would "step"—pose, often hand on hip—then repeat, for the paparazzi. As Clarissa explained how her girls would deal with clipboard lists along with security, my phone buzzed with a text. Finn.

"You like Indian?" he'd written.

"I could eat human flesh if it had tikka masala sauce on it," I zapped back.

Moments later: "LOL."

Victory! I made Finn Schiller laugh. LOL. Dyingdying-dying. I would break bread with my idol. Naan, apparently.

The next buzz came an hour later.

"Done—taking you to one of my favorite spots, Electric Lotus."

"Sooooo psyched!" I wrote back. No sooner did I hit send than I felt like a world-class doof. That's what my sister and I called dopes. I was a doof. No: I was queen of the dooves. That's the plural of *doof*. Our other favorite was "gormph." But that's only for doof-ish *guys*, and the plural is not gormves but gormphs. You can make up your own rules when you make up your own words.

Then, for the next couple hours, nothing. Pas de vibration. I felt like a foolish idiot middle-schooler checking incessantly. I was in a meeting with the stationer, a hundred-year-old letterpress in Los Feliz. Normally it would be an environment that turned me on—Pantone color wheels, paper samples, industrial machines that would press our killer logo into the cardstock—but instead my mind was adrift. I nodded as if attentive as I reached my arm into my muslin tote with a silk-screened Kelly Bag on it and retrieved my fluorescent yellow–covered iPhone for a peek. Nada. Fuck! What the hell was wrong with me! I had a boyfriend! Wylie was my family. Why the hell was I compulsively checking to see if this guy—no, this rock star—was writing me! I must be delusional. I was losing my marbles, officially, I drank the

Kool-Aid, morphing from cool cat into loser plebeian fan in my four phone-checks.

I walked out of the lot of the press back to my car, shaking my head to myself. Hazel you fucking loser idiot. Snap out of it! I thought of Cher in *Moonstruck*, hoping a momentary slap could actually beat the desire out of me. As she found . . . no such luck. I got in the hot car and rolled down the windows. And then: Cosmo's moon appeared from behind the curtain of clouds. My phone buzzed just as my soul buzzed, tipsy with excitement.

I opened the message. "Sorry I've been MIA this pm— laying dwn some trcks w/ the guys. Can't wait to see you tnight."

Crack highs couldn't possibly be better. Elation. Nervously I texted back "me neither." And then another: a smiley face.

I pulled out of the driveway with a shit-eating grin beaming brighter than my fluorescent headlights, wondering what the night would have in store.

CHAPTER 13

I have too many fantasies to be a housewife.
I guess I am a fantasy.
—Marilyn Monroe

IT WAS NEARING SIX. MEETINGS FINISHED, I MEANDERED IN A daze into the early evening, like my body was an avatar controlled by remote as my real self lounged around, eating bonbons, dreaming of Finn. His music played in the car and in my head during meetings. His voice accompanied me into elevators, garages, up the steps to a front door, as if perched above my head in a cartoon bubble, all-caps reminders of clever things he said or little witticisms he rattled off with the ease of breathing.

After my last work thing—a tech run-through with the sound and lighting guy with Clarissa in a crappy vegetarian joint I'd seen on *Entourage,* I asked to be dropped off at Kira's mother ship—Beverly Hills. Whenever I visited L.A. I felt more at home on Vermont—in Silverlake or Los Feliz. But Ki and my parents preferred Rodeo Drive. I happened upon a swank salon so I wandered in, hoping to get a quick blow-dry. A little primp wouldn't kill me, right? Shit, I just never played those girlie girl games, no beauty binges, nary an Alicia Silverstone shopping spree at the mall. But Finn made me feel like a girl, not the cool tomboy the guys at work liked me for, or the normal slobby Hazel who Wylie waited for at Urban Outfitters, but a real girl. Femme it up, Kira said. Ally Sheedy, here I come.

Bingo, they had an opening. I put on the robe and was offered tea as a "washing technician" scrubbed my scalp with intoxicating apple cider–infused shampoos and cream rinses. I got it. This shit was actually fun and enjoyable. They even had a footrest for my outstretched gams.

I exited feeling like a million bucks. I hoped it wouldn't get addictive, I could get used to this, like my sister with her weekly standing appointments at Frédéric Fekkai. I drove back to my hotel where I tried to figure out what to wear, eventually settling on my same jeans but this time a slightly more feminine white lace blouse with piping of black velvet ribbons around the short sleeves. It was Edwardian granny-chic but remained a tad sexy, due to my black cami underneath. I exhaled in front of the mirror. Less is more, I thought. Especially 'cause Finn was used to Hooters Girls and the like. Better to be myself. Better to be demure. Better to keep him guessing.

"You look beautiful," he said as I hopped in the passenger side as he stood next to the open door.

"Oh, thanks," I replied, blushing a little.

He got back in the car and gunned out of the driveway, flying down the streets in his small Porsche. Normally it was what Wylie and I called an SPC, Small Penis Car, but somehow Finn had a Get Out of Jail Free Card because he was an actual rock star whereas all other douche bags who drove expensive sports cars were merely trying to look like one.

"I love L.A.," I said, staring out the window. "I don't know why everyone in New York L.A. bashes for sport."

"Well, it's not as sophisticated, for one," Finn said. "I love living here but I have this insatiable urge to travel. I hate staying in one place for too long. I must've descended from nomads or something; I'm one of those people who just needs to be on the move. Especially if this is my base. I miss Europe too much. Asia."

"I could see that. If it's just sunshine and convertibles forever," I replied. "Daisy Dukes, bikinis on top."

"That part's not so bad," he joked with a wink. "But even I know there's a dark side here if you look for it. And you don't have to look too hard."

So weird! I'd thought that exact thing before a million times.

"My theory has always been that New York admits to its dark side in its weather and gray pavement and people on top of each other," I explained, surveying the lights. "Whereas there's just as much of it here but it's all sunglasses and cherry red cars and boobie implants, but it's smoke and mirrors. There's just as much competition and relentless drive, it's just cruising beneath the surface, which makes it creepier. I do like how New York wears its edge on its sleeve."

We drove the opening credits of the *Entourage* strip complete with tacky signage and dizzying downward views of orange-lit lights and rooftops as far as I could see.

"That is a very good theory, New York is more openly hostile and then you're happily surprised when people are nice and warm, whereas here you think of it as friendly but there's just as much hostility," he said. "If not more. Someone pats you on the back but they're pissing down your leg."

"I just think of *L.A. Story* where all the weatherman has

to do is shove up some magnetic suns with shades on. Sun!
Sun! Sun!" I said in a singsongy mock-happy voice. "But I
love the rainy days. People here freak like it's fucking acid
falling on their hairdos."

"I love when it's cold here. I fuckin' hate sweating my
balls off. But I hate freezing them off, too."

"Yeah, well. I can see that. If you didn't grow up with
seasons. I mean, even I'm dreading going back to my coat
and scarves and hats and Rudolph nose."

"How long are you here until?" he asked.

"I leave tomorrow," I lamented, suddenly. "But I'm back
again in two weeks and then for the event two weeks after
that. I'm sooo excited to see this space of yours."

"Should we go now or after dinner?"

"Whatever you want!"

"I'm starving."

Yay, I was, too. Desperately.

CHAPTER 14

*Without this playing with fantasy no creative work
has ever yet come to birth. The debt we owe to the play
of the imagination is incalculable.*

—Carl Gustav Jung

WE WENT INSIDE THE DIMLY LIT RESTAURANT WHERE HE GOT
a hero's welcome from the staff and a corner nook, where
we were seated on the floor on these cool pillows. It sounds
weird but was actually cool and foreign and felt like we were
on some kind of trip. Which I was.

We talked about other places in the city he loved, including some trendy tapas bar. He loved the mini paella cakes.

"Oh, I thought you said topless." I laughed, almost spit-
ting out my papadum.

"I know, it always sounds like that!" He chortled. "Someone should actually open a topless tapas bar. Called Topless
Tapas."

"Oh my god, that's genius! Let's totally open that!" I
squealed. "We would mint money!" Not that he needed it.

"We'd love another bottle of wine, please, Anju," Finn
asked the pierced waiter. "We have to come up with fun
dishes and cocktails for our menu. Put the cock in the cocktails," he said. "Like Mojitoesucker."

I almost spat out my Rioja. "Okay, this is hilarious. This is big time. Move over, Hooters!"

"So where do you like to eat in New York?" he asked.

Fuck. Okay . . . here was a perfectly organic, opportune time to introduce Wylie.

"Um, well . . . my uh, boyfriend is a personal chef, actually—"

"Oh, well that must be nice," he said. I couldn't read his face but he seemed blasé about Wylie's existence. "So you don't even have to leave the apartment!"

"Well, we do, still, but he cooks at home a lot, too. He, um, actually has one client, this hedge fund family on Fifth Avenue, that is so into his food that they want to invest in a restaurant for him with some big New York restaurateurs. So, it looks like that might happen pretty soon, but it's not, like, definite or anything."

"Well, ask them how they feel about a nudie Mexican chain. I think our idea has legs. Long ones."

"Yeah, and boobs."

"Here's to our business venture," he joked, raising his newly poured glass to meet mine.

I felt calmer and happy; Kira was right; it felt good to get out there—not that he would ever think of me as anything other than the lap-barfer from the airplane. We giggled over new Topless Tapas menu offerings, and the mood was light and even straight-up fun. It's not like I ever lost sight of the fact that I was drinking with my idol, but there was a sweetness and pure fun that infused our pillowed perch. Was I becoming friends with Finn Schiller?

He ordered a second bottle of wine and we clinked refilled glasses as the food came. And nothing I've ever tasted had ever been so delicious.

CHAPTER 15

One supreme fact which I have discovered is that
it is not willpower, but fantasy-imagination that creates.
Imagination is the creative force.
Imagination creates reality.
—Richard Wagner

SATED AND SLIGHTLY TIPSY, WE DROVE OFF FROM THE
dinner, and I thanked him for such a lovely time.

"It's not over yet, I have to show you my special secret
lair for your big party."

We cruised toward the mini-skyline of downtown Los
Angeles, which was obviously dwarfed by comparison to
my hometown but stood like an imposing metropolis when
cut and pasted against the teeny-tinily scaled local architecture. A few minutes later we pulled down a street that didn't
look very Angelino to me. It was exactly what my mind's
eye had fantasized about—huge warehouses with tons of
windows, an industrial, edgy vibe with an urban brick-built
strength. We got out of the car in front of the most amazing

of the buildings and walked inside the huge antique metal sliding door.

"Holy shit," I marveled. The ceiling had to've been fifty feet high, all the interior had been gutted from the days of chocolate bars past.

"Veruca Salt, eat your heart out," I said, gaping at the massive space.

"It's fuckin' cool, right?"

He walked me across the cavern of gray moonlit space over to the windows where a metal spiral staircase to nowhere hung above us.

"You could put a DJ up there," he suggested. "Just bring in some machine or forklift and he can spin from the loft."

"Infuckingcredible," I marveled. I saw it all unfold. The lights, the crowd, the jaws falling to the paved floor in unison. The promotion.

"What about press, is it okay to have all the—"

"Absolutely. Whatever you need."

"Really? Finn . . . this is so perfect, I couldn't have dreamed up a better location for this—"

"Good, it's yours, then."

"We're honestly more than happy to compensate you."

"Please. Now *I'm* gonna barf. It's fine."

"Okay," I said, looking down bashfully as I got a good glance at his hot Edward Scissorhandsian leather fencing jacket. Breathe, Hazel.

I watched as Finn's eyes narrowed as he caught sight of the antique locket around my neck. Finn reached over and barely dusted the skin on my collarbone with his fingers as he lifted the heart-shaped mini-diptych.

"*H*," he said, simply, after deciphering the extremely calligraphic thus virtually illegible letter engraved on the surface. As he held it delicately in his left hand, he took his

right index finger and gently ran it over the curves and ser-
aphs of my ornate initial, following the gentle tracks of the
burin, then looking up into my unblinkable eyes. "It's just
beautiful," he said, studying it.

"It was my grandmother's," I stammered. "I was named
for her."

"What's inside?"

"Uh . . . nothing, actually."

"Nothing?" he said, lifting his eyes from the charm to
meet mine.

"I know, it's weird," I admitted with a shrug. "I didn't
really know what to put in it, so it's just empty."

To my utter shock he slowly leaned down toward his
hand, and as my lungs were unable to squeeze out the CO_2,
he put his lips to my locket. He kissed it. And in doing so
thieved about five beats of my pulse. He stood back up and
looked at me with his searing blue eyes.

"I'm not allowed to kiss your mouth, so I'll kiss your
heart."

Lightning bolt chucked down by Zeus himself electrified
my entire being. In that moment, as he let my necklace gently
fall from his fingertips back to my clavicle, Finn pressed the
pause button on my entire respiratory system. I could barely
gather the thoughts let alone the words to make their way to
my tongue, so my hand simply found itself taking his. I gave
it a doting squeeze then turned away toward the door. "We
should go," I said as my pulse shot through the cavernous
ceiling. "I have an early flight."

"All right, H."

"Sorry," I offered, not quite knowing why.

"No need to be," he said, with a warm, sincere smile.
"Anyway," he added. "You'll be back soon enough."

CHAPTER 16

*I don't want to see pictures of Hollywood stars in their
dressing gowns taking out the rubbish. It ruins the fantasy.*
—Sarah Brightman

THIS TIME, THE PLANE FLEW STEADILY THROUGH THE CRYS-
tal blue skies, visibility thousands of miles, liftoff glorious.
But if my head were any gauge, it was as if we were flying
through the tumbling tumult once again, bumpy and in free
fall, nauseating and flirting with ashen sprinklage on some
rectangular red state in the middle.

It was Finn's fault. Fuck. He kept popping up on my
screen like a hidden point in one of Badass's video games—a
pixilated pot of gold, a secret weapon stashed in a hidden
closet door, a bonus round in life. I tried to highlight and
delete him from my brain, only for him to pop up again. And
soon enough, somewhere over Utah, I found myself fantasiz-
ing about him ravishing me. My problems with him were
myriad, though the crux lay tied up in this paradox: Finn
brought out the best and the worst in me. He elicited a brilliant streak; I was much funnier with him, more clever, on

a quicker setting than normal. He turned me on, not just sexually, okay that, too, but literally, like a new bulb was installed, I burned brighter, stronger. I was so excited by his larger-than-life presence that perhaps I dug deeper, tried harder, was super-Hazel, Good Witch Hazel, Super Me. Though quite honestly it all seemed to flow naturally with zero effort. He just sparked me to be better, like a worthy tennis opponent luring out the aces inside you. If I were a witch, it was he that gave me my wand. And I couldn't stop thinking about his wand.

But then there was the dark side. The naughty witch. A Kansas house should fall on me for daydreaming of Finn when I was totally taken. And in love! Wylie was Kansas . . . he was my head, my heart, my courage . . . my home. He was everything to me, the real life I always wanted to open my eyes to after a bad dream, exhaling in dulcet relief that he was beside me.

But here was the thing about Kansas. There was no color. Not that Wylie was gray and blah—he wasn't at all— but Finn was like the first time I'd seen fluorescents. I went to Day-Glo instantly on that flight. But while Finn made me sharper, he also brought out many of the seven deadly sins and the stark colors that accompany them. Green greed, for one. For more time with him, another text, an e-mail, a sighting, another scavenged moment to connect. And for jealousy, of the girls who shared his bed, got inside, even the ones who scissored his heart to smithereens. I wish I could have been there, in his more innocent times, leading him down a different path, one that showed him how much love can make it all better rather than worse. And let's not even speak of Lust. Passionate purple like the quivering arrow from *A Midsummer Night's Dream* whose errant bull's-eye of a lily-white flower rendered it violent violet. Yes, I loved

Wylie. He was my cam, my touchstone. My all-clear on the Doppler 5000. But there it was: an all-encompassing storm that made me shiver with desire for Finn. And what was sunshine without the storms? The truth is this: I felt more alive than ever before. Even if tortured, I felt woken up. My stomach did a loop-de-loop just like my westbound flight. I gripped the armrests as if we'd taken a deep dip, when we hadn't. I opened my eyes and realized the ghost of Finn next to me was making me feel like a shooting star, not the metal bird I was flying inside. I closed my eyes again. I wondered how it'd feel if I had let him kiss me in that warehouse. I mentally pressed the rewind button, dreaming of his lips on mine, as he held me in his strong enormous arms. I had looked up all his lyrics on the Internet, even though I knew most of them, and even in the absence of his throaty voice and pummeling guitars, his words set me afire. Especially as I imagined him writing them in a fury of prolific inspiration. Cut to my hotel room. I pictured him there, lying next to me where I slept alone. I imagined what he would be like, his tattooed arms around me, my hands in his black hair, his warm mouth that sang such hemlock-dipped words. Of course he'd be wildly different from Wylie, violent maybe. I probably couldn't even keep up, given that I'm not incredibly prone to kink, being somewhat of a control freak and not wanting to succumb to blindfolds or wrists tied to bedposts, both of which have been featured in his videos. I'd probably be boring to him, no matter how fevered my grip of his back, no matter how high-speed my breaths. I could moan and kiss and bite with the best of 'em but I'm sure the courtesan types who fucked him rotten would find my sheet style positively junior varsity. I'm just not that exciting. Basic sex excites me enough.

It seemed every hour my thoughts were flooded with

images of us having sex, in the airplane bathroom, the warehouse, his tinted-windowed car. Maybe I could be the antidote for his years of pounding poison. Maybe I could make it all better. Maybe I could show Finn that within that crushed hollow rib cage he sings about, there is a chance to feel again.

Wait . . . WTF?!?!?! I had Wylie! See, this is why fantasies are wrong. Wrong! How can I let my mind go adrift and wandering like this? Too crazy. Okay . . . Hazel, I told myself. *You love Wylie.* He is the greatest guy on the face of the earth. You have built a life together. You once had lust for him like this . . . right? Yeah! I think. Yes, of course you did. I thought back to my first kisses with Wylie, Robert Doisneau–rivaling, passionate, beautiful. He'd cooked me dinner and walked me to get a taxi home. He'd gallantly flagged one for me and we high-fived over the score of a coveted van cab. And then after he'd opened the door, he took my hand and pulled me into him, kissing me so softly and deftly, it was as if I'd never been kissed. The ghosts of all boyfriends past faded into the black hours of the early morning with that kiss. Our tongues sweetly searched each other's as I put my arms around him and squeezed him, my fingers searching his hair dotingly as he parted, panting and aglow.

But there was Finn, walking in stage left. Out of nowhere, I fantasized we were in the warehouse again, but this time, I'd push him against the wall and kiss him, pulling off his jacket and running my hands down his back. I'd make love to him like in his song, lovingly and violently, his words and notes throbbing in my ears, my entire body awakened in a desire for him that was so intense it clouded my every thought. The plane's takeoff? Didn't notice. Some turbulence? Who cares. I used to wish to hasten each painful step of travel, the grody food placed in front of us, the clearing of said food, the dumbass *Mighty Ducks 4* crap that played on the screens. I would flip through *SkyMall* or do a stupid in-flight magazine crossword, anything anything to make this time go faster. But not this time. I stared at the hideous airplane fabric upholstery on the seat in front of me as I zoned into a reverie of Finn. What I would do to him. What I'd give up this time. If he'd have me. We had connected, even just in unspeakable chemistry . . . or was it in my head? It felt real when he held my hand momentarily. I could perhaps pull it off. How far we'd get I had no idea, but my crush on him was so intense I hoped I could at the very least scratch the itch once. To know what it was like to taste him, run my hands down his ribs, through his black hair. I knew from how his body racked with fierce breaths in something so tame as a song that in sex he would positively destroy the mattress, feathers afloat from his animalistic quest for pleasure. I ran my hand down my neck, dreaming it was his palm on my veins, his fingers walking their way to my head. I got chills from my hallucination. I felt the chill turn to a hot flash, which surged through my whole body, knowing I was fired up more by the illusion of Finn on top of me than I ever had been in real life. Maybe I couldn't handle a guy like him. Maybe I'd melt into a puddle to be spatula'd off the cement floor. Whatever the reality may bring, I clung to my closed-eyed reveries. So much so that I could barely handle deplaning, baggage claim, and navigating arrivals terminal hell, not because of the hordes or the racket but because it all required my eyes to be open. Thank god for the time change, which catapulted me into night as I hit New York and the lights of JFK. When the wheels hit the tarmac I officially realized I was a mess. In Los Angeles, my moral elasticity was like when you overspend in Monopoly—it was a game, so who cares? But now I was home. In "real life." In my territory. In the streets I'd walked with my boyfriend and love. And yet . . . I couldn't wait to get in bed just so I could lie down and not have to face the glaring light of day and the realities it held. The only place I wanted to go was fetal position in my bed. Under the covers, secure and cozy with my reveries. Seventh row center in the movie theater within my head. Watching the film that starred Finn and me.

I got home to find some supper waiting for me in the fridge with a cute note from Wy, who was cooking for a client that night. I felt a twinge of guilt as I looked at his adorable handwriting, the hand that felt familiar from years of Post-its on nights of missed intersections when he'd leave to cater a dinner before I came home. Dear heart.

Before flopping on my bed, I went to take a shower, and when I emerged, I quickly glanced at my phone. My pulse pounded with three little words: *New. Text. Message:* "Wanted to make sure you got home safe, little witch." Bingo. Somehow my moral compass quivered, as if clutched by a magnetic schizo seizure, like *War of the Worlds*. All the warm feelings engendered by Wy's Tupperware'd meal and precious note were somehow eclipsed by Finn's soul-searing check-in. My quiet inner-cinematographer gulped. Action.

CHAPTER 17

A restaurant is a fantasy—a kind of living fantasy in which diners are the most important members of the cast.
—Warner LeRoy

THE NEXT DAY I WOKE UP AND GOT DRESSED FOR WORK, tiptoeing to let Wylie sleep, but then wanted to have some form of communication that didn't involve a pen.

"Babe?" I whispered gently in his slumbering ear. "Babe, I'm leaving for work. I loved my scallion pancakes and smoked salmon, honeykins, thank you."

I could tell by his comatose state that he must've come in really late. I was just about to back away slowly when I heard him mutter two virtually unintelligible whispered words: "human blanket."

I was almost at the door and frankly a bit warm in my jacket, but I obliged, per our tradition. I lay down on top of him and smashed him into the Tempur-Pedic. We always did it when we were not overlapping in waking hours and if one had to sneak off, we'd always at least stop for a human blanket.

"Ahhhhhhh, my FAVORITE," he said, this time clearer.

"Hi, Wyliekins."

"Hi," he said, eyes still closed. "Wait, lemme look at you, Velcro."

He rolled over and opened his big brown peepers. He really was James Franco–esque. "Beautiful girl," he said, drunk on fatigue. "Welcome home."

We sometimes called each other Velcro 'cause when we had started dating we literally would stay adhered to each other in bed Sunday mornings until our tummies were growling so much we had to get up to eat.

I smiled and patted his head on the down pillow.

"Missed you."

"You didn't check in enough," he said, not accusatorily but kind of needily.

I exhaled. "Babe, I was crazed. You know you were never not with me." Lies.

"Haze, you're my family," he said.

Fuck. Pang of guilt scissored my guts, but at the same time a tsunami of claustrophobia crashed over me.

"Shoot, honey, I have to go, I'm late." I leaned over and kissed his forehead. "I love you."

"Love you so."

I walked out and when I got in the street, after fishing my MetroCard out of my messenger bag, my first order of business was a phone check.

Nuthin.

Fuck!

Before crashing, I had texted back "How chivalrous . . . here safe and sound xoH," which ever-so-slightly upped the flirtation ante with the casual insertion of kiss/hug, but it was benign and common in my e-mails to everyone; it was so routine I literally wrote it to my Poland Spring delivery service guy. For some reason I started to panic when there was no sign of life. Wait . . . was I totally delusional?! I was A NOBODY AND HE WAS A GRAMMY-WINNING quote unquote "RECORDING ARTIST." Was I just some insane dysmorphic freak who was so swept up in fantasy she couldn't get a grip? Oh my god . . . was I like those fat people who line up for model-search auditions? Shit.

I walked to the station and hopped on the L train to Brooklyn, got my morning iced coffee at Blue Bottle in Williamsburg, which Noah also frequented, though he rather grossly announced he doesn't take his first sip until he sees the front door of the office because if he so much as sniffs it he can feel the intestines a-chuggin'. Nice. Basically it's the equivalent of Roto-Rooter for humans. Also known as the SNL fauxmercial sketch ColonBlow. I walked to the office and arrived early enough that most of my colleagues hadn't yet cruised in on their skateboards, motorcycles, Segways, or some other mildly alternative mode of transport.

I sat down at my desk, and while I was catching up on all the e-mails I'd blown off in California my phone buzzed.

"Guess what my 1st thought of the day was?" read the text. Finn!

"What?" I wrote back.

"Menu item #1 for Topless Tapas. QuesaDDillas."

I howled at my desk as people started to meander in.

"GENIUS."

Fuck, I loved him. I was texting with a fucking ROCK STAR. Okay . . . I rubbed my hands together mentally, gotta add to the game here. Lightbulb.

"Chips platter: I'm Nacho Bitch."

I waited for his response.

Shwing!

"LOL!!!!!!!!" he replied.

"Haze, whatcha got?" Noah asked, entering in his normal Tasmanian devil flurry. "Brad, Mike, Severin, Paco, conference room." He walked by all of us, and we obediently rose from our various areas, following him to the all-glass-and-steel room overlooking the river.

"Boss in—gotta bolt, more in a bit," I texted Finn.

We went into the room, each plopping on a sleekly designed-yet-ergonomically correct three-thousand-dollar-but-doesn't-look-it swivel chair Noah had had flown in from Copenhagen.

"How was California?" Noah asked as everyone took their seats.

"Insane," I pronounced. "I'm glad you're all sitting down. 'Cause you're gonna faint."

I've always had a flair for the dramatic, what can I say?

"Out with it!" Sev demanded.

I began with a description of my harrowing yet heavenly flight. The barf, the comfort, the convo, and the denouement at LAX.

My office mates were literally on the edge of the $3,000 ergonomic seats Noah had proffered after his yogi touted their praises.

"He's literally obsessed with our stuff. He plays it all the time at home and on the road with his band and he freaked when I said we were doing our launch in L.A. this time. And when I said I was touring raw spaces downtown he offered me his building."

"Just like that?" Paco asked, incredulous.

"Just like that," I gloated. "And at no charge."

"Finn Schiller has a building?" Mike asked. "Why?"

"I don't know. Real estate investment, maybe potential empire headquarters for The Void empire? The point is, it's ours. And it rocks."

"No way he wants no dough," Noah probed, leaning back in his chair.

"Goose egg. Gratis," I said, hand raised, as if in a witness booth. "All he wants is to bring a few friends."

"Wait a second . . . are you saying he'd come?!" Sev asked, mouth agape.

"Holy shit!" Noah beamed. "Good going, Haze! I'm so psyched you puked your little brains out! That's for taking one for the team."

He leaned across the conference table and high-fived me.

We went over other logistics and the meeting wrapped with a huge pat on the back for yours truly.

After a flurry of editor phone calls and fine-tuning a press release, my phone buzzed with a text.

"Chicken Flautata's."

I giggled in my chair. My creative juices were flowing. My turn.

"Enchilaaaahhhhdas."

I went back to my computer until he TM'd me again a half hour later "for our COCKtail menu: Tres Equis beer XXX."

I was pulled into a meeting with the design department, but as they showed me options, my wheels were turning.

"Shimmychangas" I surreptitiously sent him under the table.

I went to lunch with Brad, who actually was a sick guitar player in his own right, and snuck a couple peeks at my phone.

The first was another addition to our cocktails ("SIN-gria") and then the next made my heart skip a beat. "What date are you coming back, bewitching girl?"

"What's wrong?" Brad asked as he saw my eyes widen into saucers.

"Oh, uh, nothing. Let's go back to the office."

I called my sister, asking if I could come up and see my nieces and have a much-needed drink, I had deets to download and craved her advice.

"Anytime," she said, almost begging. "You know the corkscrew hits the pinot noir the second the door closes behind my nanny."

I texted back Finn with the dates for my next trip, plus one more for good measure (Sopa de Whoretilla—not my best, I know), and within minutes he wrote back that we would have dinner that night. Then another buzz.

"And I'd love to scoop you up from LAX if you don't have a ride."

I was breathless. I thought I was going to explode. Because of his text flurry, including what he was up to and the weather there, my day flew by. Work was actually a blast, and because he was so into what we were doing at Badass, suddenly, so was I. It was like he renewed my vigor for what I do every day, just when it was getting monotonous.

CHAPTER 18

You know you're in love when you can't fall asleep
because reality is finally better than your dreams.
—Dr. Seuss

I BLEW OUT OF THERE AT FIVE ON THE DOT, FEELING LIKE I
was going to explode. I couldn't go home. I just started walking. And walking. My legs led me to the Brooklyn Bridge, a
place I love to stroll, often with thoughts as heavy as the steel
girders supporting it. I felt like someone had shot a cannon
through my midsection, but just like the liquid metal *Terminator 2* guy, it kept closing so no one could see it. But the
scar, the pain is still there, even though the oozing silver fills
it to the naked eye. The memory of the hollowness haunted
me as I put a hand to my tummy, as if to prove to myself I'm
still actually me because I feel so utterly changed.

I've had butterflies. Everyone has. First days of school, a
new job, a budding romance. But this wasn't a giddy Aurora
in the woods singing with bluebirds abuzz on love shitting
on her fucking shoulder. This was different . . . better . . .
worse. Because the drama factor was spiked so high, thanks

to the Squeeze song forbidden fruit aspect. Each step I took felt like the last before a high jump in the Olympics, or a plummet with a bungee cord. Or an aerial like those psycho X Games people. Ever since I'd returned home, each forced bite of food felt like a Last Supper before the electric chair and then the next was like filet mignon after wandering the desert drinking cactus juice. I was officially a mess. A beautiful mess.

The astonishing thing about hitting a milestone birthday is that on some level, you feel like you've crossed a finish line, arrived. But I think the pit of despair and mystery of life widens when it dawns on you, with a vertebrae-tingling chill, that you never "arrive." It's always the run before the high jump. After any medal ceremony there can always be another and another. You can always get better or, gasp . . . grow. I thought I was done growing up, or at least had chosen to not grow up. But I had my perfect life and now I actively felt myself changing, morphing from all that I was even a month ago. And it hurt. Like the cannon. And now I realize why they call it growing pains. Kirk Cameron (who I heard is now a Bible thumper) and the gang were onto something.

Just then Wylie called.

"Hi, babe!" I said, at once happy to hear his cute chirp but also feeling oddly like my wings-of-fantasy flight had been clipped by reality.

"Hi, sweet pea," he said. "I miss you . . ."

"Me, too."

"I feel like I've barely seen you and you're leaving again. I want to cook for us, but my boss is entertaining like crazy."

"That's because they know they're losing you soon! They want to impress all their friends before you bolt," I suspected aloud.

"Nah, they've been so great, and last night they brought

me out and told the guests they would be backing me and they all oohed and ahhed and stuff."

"Any ideas for the name yet?" I probed.

"A couple . . . ," he teased. "Oh shit, that's them—I'll call you later, honey."

"Bye, Wy," I said. "I love you."

So now what? My control freak self was in unchartered territory. Do I flush thoughts of Finn out of my brain? I tried . . . but then I'd reach for my phone to see if he'd texted. But it made me feel good to rewind and play the film stills of our cinematic movie flight together. It felt like a small little black-and-white photography flip book in my mind's hand that I could buzz through with super 8–style haziness, then flip it again to reveal a new moment, and another: his hand on my back, his saying there was no one like me, his jacket creaking as he moved. I felt the pit in my stomach return, that unfillable hole. As much as I tried to brush it off and walk through the motions of my evening without dwelling on its growing presence, deep down I suspected that it would haunt me until I threw down ropes, rappelled to its core, and explored it further.

I arrived on 212 soil and called Kira.

"Hi, I'm two blocks away," I said, panting. "I need to see you."

"Come on over."

The subway I'd taken might as well have been a rocket ship crafted by Houston NASA dorks. When I detrained on Seventy-seventh Street, I was in another universe: the Upper East Side. My sister lived on a tree-lined block on Fifth Avenue facing Central Park. The leafy vista was so calming and serene and my nieces, Iris and Maeve, were still in their adorable hunter green Chapin pinafores with Peter Pan collars when I arrived.

"HAZEL!!!!!!" Iris shrieked, flying into my arms with a leap worthy of Usain Bolt.

"Hi, gals!" I said, kissing each on the head.

Kira came out, already sipping her vino, which she did crack precisely at 4:59 with her Rabbit bottle opener, right as the nanny headed home to Queens. Sometimes Vern's coat isn't even on when Kira's unwrapped the foil over the cork.

"Hi, Ki," I said, kissing her. "I'll take one of those. Or four."

The girls went off to play a bit before dinner, and my sister and I plopped on her delicious sofa, legs curled up, facing each other, wineglasses in hand.

"Talk to me," she said.

I took a deep breath.

"Wylie is proposing," I said, the air almost trapped in my lungs as I sputtered it out.

Kira didn't react. "You don't seem too off-the-wall excited about that . . . ," she observed.

I described my ceiling revelation.

"Oh shit," she said, taking a swig.

"Kira, I love him. I do. I really do—he is the sweetest, most devoted, most loving guy. I mean, they don't make them like this. He tells me he loves me with all his heart and all his soul. I almost feel like if I didn't say yes, it would destroy him."

"Don't be so conceited. I know you're fabulous, but he is, too, and he'd be fine."

"Yeah, you're right," I said, knowing my boyfriend was such a catch he'd be gobbled up by the single-girl piranhas that swarmed New York.

"What the fuck is wrong with me?" I asked her. "He's so smart, so gorgeous, he's an incredible and probably soon-to-be illustrious chef. He's got it all!"

"So why are you worried?" she asked, eyebrow raised. She knew me so well and read my indecision.

"Because I can't stop thinking about Finn."

"You just met him."

"I know! I'm being ridiculous. Maybe this is all in my head, who knows."

"I know it's not," Kira said. "You're always the girl who says the guy doesn't like you, doesn't notice you, even when they do. You must be on to something."

"Kira," I started slowly. "I know this is going to sound so cocky and so absurd but . . . there's this . . . crazy weird tension with Finn. It's fun and there's chemistry and it's real. I feel like . . . we have this thing. This instant, deep connection. My stomach is filled with butterflies, and they are going shithouse in there."

"I can tell," Kira replied.

"You know his song 'Beautiful Mess'?" I asked Kira.

"Of course. We played it on a loop that summer on the Vineyard scooping ice cream. When I had one huge arm and one skinny one."

"Okay, well, that's him. He's gorgeous and fierce and strong but also deeply anguished and broken. And I want to glue him back together."

"Oh nonononono," she said, shaking her head like the mommy she was. "Nooooo."

"Why? What?"

"Hell to the hell to the HELL to the no. *GLUE?* That is a very dangerous word."

"Why?"

"What is glue used for, Elmer?"

"Making things."

"Or fixing things. Broken things. The worst thing a woman can ever think is that she can heal a man. He is not

Humpty Dumpty. You are not going to 'fill him' or complete him like the deaf people in *Jerry Maguire*."

"I disagree. It's like *The Missing Piece*," I said, reminding her of our absolute favorite childhood book. "The Pac-Man–shaped thing is literally able to roll when he gets his pie-shaped missing piece. It makes him whole, makes him speed up, see the world from a whole new perspective."

"Hazel. Have you read it recently? Because I just read it to Maeve. You obviously don't remember the ending."

"Whatever. This is stupid. The point is Shel Silverstein was a fucking genius and I learned more from his books than I did from that mountain of crap in college," I blazed. "I can't believe you're not happy for me. I'm having dinner with our IDOL!"

"I am happy, Haze. I just love you. To pieces. No pun."

"I know."

"I want to protect you, and I know I can't. No one can impart wisdom to the lovesick. No one. Not sisters, not Shel Silverstein, not the fascist religious regime that dictates moral propriety. You have to make your own mistakes, and pay for them, or not."

"What's your point?" I asked her, confused.

"My point is that no one can guide you here. It's the hardest thing, that draw. That pull . . ."

"How do you know?"

I heard Kira exhale.

"Because . . . I know what it feels like. A few years back. I fell, for about a month, madly in love with this guy."

I was stunned. "WHAT? You cheated on Drew?"

"No, no. I didn't. Nothing happened. Chaste all the way. But we became fast friends—totally randomly, I wandered into a little shop in the East Village and bought a woodcut in a vintage frame, and he took my e-mail for when new ones came in from Dublin. We started e-mailing and it got more and more intense and I realized I started having these crazy fantasies about him."

"Ki, are you serious? Why didn't you tell me?"

"Because. It was wrong. Normal, natural even, maybe, but *wrong*. I adore my husband. He gave me my daughters, my family, but this man tripped a wire inside me and absolutely set my chest cavity on fire."

"So what did you do?"

"I decided I could either have an affair with him, which would probably peter out and have me suffocate on guilt for betraying my adorable teddy bear of a husband, or I could do what people do: put all those emotions in a box, reach up high on my mental stepladder, and put it up on the top shelf on my brain's Manhattan Mini Storage."

"So that's it? You just broke off communication?"

"Mm-hmm. I mean, I told him I needed to, and he understood. And you know what? I felt a sad tug on my aorta for a little while, but soon enough it was like being on a sailboat and slowly drifting away from land, leaving the sand behind you. It became farther and farther away, and in the end, that lust, that longing, was replaced by relief. Absolute relief that I was grown-up enough not to jeopardize the thing that means the most to me in the world: my family."

"Wow."

"Yeah. It was intense."

"So . . . do you think if I hook up with Finn I will always regret it with Wylie?"

"Only you can figure that out."

"If I sail away from Finn, I just know I'd dive overboard and swim back. I have to kiss him. I have to."

"Then go for it. And don't beat yourself up."

"First I need to press the pause button with Wylie."

"Just be really really careful," she advised. "I don't want you to do anything you'd regret."

"That's my worry," I confessed. "But I'll talk to him. I just need to stave off an engagement while I work out what I really want. I just don't know if I can be . . . Velcro'd forever. That feels like such a long time. I don't think I'm ready."

"I just hope he's willing to wait," said Kira. "He's been wanting to get married for a while."

"I know. That's what I'm afraid of."

CHAPTER 19

All cartoon characters and fables must be exaggeration,
caricatures. It is the very nature of fantasy and fable.
—Walt Disney

MOST WOMEN ARRIVE HOME TO FIND THEIR GUY'S ON THE
pot or an armchair but mine was inevitably in the kitchen.
From the attosecond I inserted my key into our lock, I was
seized with the intoxicating scent of food cooking. Wylie's
XM rock station Liquid Metal blared, as a symphony of
whisks and metal bowls and oven doors accompanied the
pummeling riffs.

"BABE!" he said, dropping his incredible-smelling coq
au vin to run and give me a huge hug. Fuck he was adorable.
"I missed you so much, honey. I'm sorry I was dead to the
world when you left, I wish you'd've woken me up!"

"I know, baby, but you were all cozy sound asleep love-
bug! I didn't wanna disturb you."

"You always can, you know that. I prefer you to sleep."

"YUM, that looks sooooo good."

"It'll be ready in a few."

He poured me a glass of Bordeaux.

"Holy shit, this is incredible!"

"The Pantzers gave it to me last night to thank me," he said. "I made this wild mushroom menu with soup and *sotto-cenare* lasagna and salad with this white truffle oil dressing and they freaked out."

"Oh god, that sounds amazing," I told him.

I set our little nook, a table for two, with our vintage plates and hotel silver and lit the two small Juliska hurricane lamps Kira bought us for Christmas.

We ate his delicious concoction, and he told me that he'd just found out that day that his restaurant was greenlit. The owner of the restaurant where he was sous chef would back him and be his partner. They would begin looking for spaces right away. In our neighborhood, no less.

"HONEY, that's AMAZING!" I said. I got up out of my chair to hug him. He pulled me down on his lap and kissed me.

"Congrats, I always knew this would happen. You're gifted and have your own unique style and I love every morsel and everyone else will, too, babe."

"It's all coming together," he said, his melted Hershey's kiss eyes smiling. "Everything's moving along perfectly," he added, squeezing me. "And everyone loves the name."

"You found the name?"

"No. You did."

"Me?"

"Hazel."

"What?"

"No, the name. Hazel. Everyone digs it."

"Oh sweethear . . ." My voice trailed off, seized by guilt. "I can totally see that in all-caps in Zagat."

"I thought so, too!" he said, taking my hand.

He leaned in and kissed me.

Enter Finn. Almost like in the peripheries of my cerebral cortex, walking along those spongy brain squiggles, as if on a balance beam, teetering into view. I pulled away and looked at my boyfriend's gorgeous face. And felt so removed and distant. I walked back to my side and sat down, looking at my lap.

"What's wrong?" he asked, sensing from my mailed-in kiss that I was elsewhere.

"I'm so happy for you. I just want that same feeling of peace for me. And I don't . . . have it. Things're just . . . so crazy at work. With the launch and stuff."

"I thought everything was great," he said, breaking off a piece of caramelized onion bread. "Noah would die without you. You're his fucking lifeline."

"I guess," I said, drawing breath nervously. "I just, um, I kinda want everything to just slow down and like calm a bit. In general."

"Like what, you mean work stuff?"

"No. Everything—I just feel a little bit like I'm so frantic and I've been running around like a headless chicken for two years now and it's great but I kind of keep having these fantasies of like a desert island. Or Paris. Or just, Mars, I don't know."

Wylie looked a little concerned. "Well, what about here? I mean . . . with me?"

I looked at him but didn't speak quickly enough to quash the spark of worry in his eyes.

"Wylie, I love you so much. I do. I just . . . I'm really not ready to settle down yet. I'm just not. I'm sorry, I know we've talked about it but I'm just . . . not in a great place right now."

He paused, sipping his wine.

He didn't seem totally shocked.

"I know, I can tell," he said. He cut another bite of chicken as I sat looking at him. "I don't know what you're waiting for, exactly," he said. "It's been three years together."

God, we were like the reverse of every other couple! Kira had to practically threaten Drew after two years with "no ring, no bring" ultimatums before she moved in. And here I was playing the loath-to-commit guy role.

"You're right, and that's my issue," I said, trying to tread carefully. "I'm not . . . a hundred percent sure. Of anything right now."

Wylie put down his fork.

"Wait a minute. You're saying you're not sure about us?" he asked, now with a stunned look.

"I'm not sure about anything; I'm just saying I'm really confused, sweetheart. I mean, I'm not confused that I love you, I do, fiercely, but I just don't feel ready to say 'I do, until death do us part' this attosecond. That's a thousandth of a nano, by the way."

"Thanks, Galileo," he deadpanned. "My question is, and this is what I want you to think about, Hazel, if you're not ready now, will you ever be ready?"

I took a deep breath, exhaling as the remorse of my wild forest-fire fantasies crept up the back of my neck. FinnFinnFinnFinn. There was no way I could not see where this would lead. If anywhere. If I wasn't a deranged fan with a crush gone awry. But what was the alternative? I wasn't Kira with the children. I was free still, to go off the road most frequently traveled. What was life but to be lived before croakage! We were all gonna be dead and buried in sixty years, and I've always been a diem carpe-ing kinda gal. I tried to wrestle with good versus evil like a cartoon angel and devil on my shoulders, but I knew damn well the pitchfork clipped the wings before I'd even hit the ground at LAX. The full-loaded fantasy freight train had left the station.

"Wylie, I don't know if I'll ever be ready. I'm just a little lost right now. I have been for a while and I just need to find my way back. I don't know how long that will take."

"And I want to help you do that, I really do," he said, shaking his head. "But I can't wait forever."

"I know." I nodded guiltily. "I just need to work some stuff out and figure out what I really want out of life. Kira was married and pregnant with her second kid at my age, but I'm so not there."

"Hazel," he said carefully. "I think . . . maybe we should take a little break so you can figure stuff out."

I felt a teeny tiny sting, but it was accompanied by a relief chaser.

He'd said it, I didn't.

"Okay," I said quietly, looking down at our West Elm brown Moroccan-style rug.

"Okay? That's it? You're not even going to fight for us?" he said, throwing his arms up. Now I could tell that was a bluff, and he was pissed.

What was wrong with me? Any girl would die to marry him!

"Wylie, I don't know what I want right now and a break might be good for us."

"Fine, Hazel. Take your break. But don't think I'll be waiting for you, holding your coat while you figure it all out."

I paused and looked around the apartment. Our apartment. That we'd decorated together with fun finds from random trips and flea market scores. I thought of all the meals we'd shared and fun times we'd had making it into our home. But the truth was, in recent months between our crazy career jugglage worthy of Ringling Brothers or Chinese plate spinning minors, we were like . . . roommates. We were ships in the (dark, stormy) night, and I felt such a pit in my stomach about hurting his sweet self. But accompanying that bitter dread was the unbridled euphoria of Finn. As Wylie continued to cook our dinner, I was basking in fantasies of our kisses, conjuring images of mad embraces over and over. I imagined Finn kissing my neck, sliding my bra strap off my shoulder, unhooking it gently as he seemed lustfully drawn to undressing me; I was so flattered by his ardor; Wy was mellower and not wildly romantic like Finn, who was tortured and bursting with emotion. Finn had a sexual avarice that was palpable when we were near each other—pure bubbling-over chemistry, the kind that burst a test tube in the science lab. Wylie was quieter and subdued; he would never rip off my blouse. But sometimes I fucking want my shredded clothes in a balled heap on the floor! I wanted to be wanted. These feelings mingled like some kind of hemlock/ecstasy cocktail—part beaming me to hell, part rocketing me to the sun, moon, and stars. I thought of Wylie's soft light brown curls. His kind eyes squinting with shock and distress as he stirred the sauce. I even feared his turning on me. And yet, Finn was somehow a sign—I mean how crazy was it that I met him flukishly close to saying his name as my celeb crush? It had to be destiny. Right? Or was that ridick. Maybe the little now drug-addicted *Terminator 2* kid was right: "no fate but what you make." Well it was time to go and make it. And like Linda Hamilton, I had to be strong. But not with veins popping out of my arms.

I practically swooned with the ambrosial scent of caramelizing onions.

I walked toward Wylie, who was pouring sherry into a bisque swimming with minced hen-of-the-woods mushrooms.

"Your favorite," he said, pulling out the 'shroom-smothered wooden spoon, offering me a taste. I took it and almost cried that it would be my last, and our eyes met.

"It's intoxicating. As usual," I said softly. "Wylie, I'm so sorry."

He shrugged almost coldly, and I could tell I had wounded his gentle soul.

"You've been withdrawing from me lately anyway," he said. "And I knew something was up when you didn't want me to come out for your launch. Maybe it's just not the right time for you to think about settling down."

"Wylie, I know myself. I would rather regret my choice than regret my lack of balls to make one."

"Well congratulations, you have balls," he said. "And you totally chopped mine off with a Wüsthof cleaver, thanks."

"Wylie, it's not about you; I'm lost right now, it's about me."

"Yeah, thanks, George Costanza, I noticed," he said. "Isn't it always, Hazel?"

He turned off the stove and walked out, gently closing the door. Just as I'd closed it on him.

He left the beautiful meal sitting there, but despite the inviting aromas, I suddenly didn't feel very hungry.

The worst part? I felt horrible that I didn't feel horrible. The fact was, I had something so much more electrifying waiting in the wings. I felt awful for sweet Wylie, but on the flip side I had to scratch this itch I had for Finn. I was possessed by longing.

As I heard the elevator door close behind him in the hallway, it ravaged a beat from my pulse, but it quickly was replaced by twenty quickened pumps as I looked to my handbag.

I grabbed it from the floor, rifled through it as if through the California dust searching for gold nuggets, and retrieved it, with my hand practically shaking. Message.

"Taking you to this incredible restaurant called Animal, you'll love it."

I paused, looking around my sweet apartment. We'd decorated it together, lugging West Elm furniture and flea market finds, splurging here and there on curtains and crystal. I took a deep breath and somehow managed to exhale the melancholy of that bittersweet space we'd inhabited.

I looked back down at the phone, with the text message sitting there. From Finn Schiller.

"My tummy's growling already, so to speak" I wrote back. I felt my forehead get hot. I think my temperature rose a decimal point with each text, and now I was in full fever mode. I was burning up for Finn, and despite Wylie's dear heart, I didn't see myself cooling off anytime soon.

CHAPTER 20

Though dreams can be deceiving,
like faces are to hearts, they serve for sweet relieving,
when fantasy and reality lie too far apart.
—Anonymous

THE NEXT TEN DAYS FLEW BY. WYLIE HAD RESUMED HIS SEMI-
Cullen schedule of vampire night gigs, and so we were con-
veniently ships in the night in the apartment. We'd pass each
other with stilted exchanges and go through the motions,
but my pounding heart was in L.A. I'd downloaded news
of our break to my sister, who was supportive yet naturally
concerned for Wylie, as they had grown to be family. But
just when she would ask after him and get my permission to
reach out to say hi to him, in the next breath she'd giddily
beg for updates about Finn. And I had plenty to spare. Our
text velocity was spiking and the length picking up characters with each zapped greeting.

I worked up a storm, fielding calls while juggling adorable texts from Finn that either cracked me up with hyena-

like laughter or made me melt into my ergochair ("I fucking can't stop thinking about you, Hazel.")

"I can't, either" I had replied.

And then, something novel.

"Can I call you?" he wrote back.

The thought hadn't occurred to me! "Sure!" Moments later my phone rang.

"Hello?" I giggled, timpani in my chest thumping.

"Hi, I almost forgot these are actual working phones!" He laughed. Oh my god. His throaty voice made me swoon.

"I know! We're like texting teens or something."

"Seriously," he said, pausing. "Hazel . . . I don't know what it is about you, but you make me feel like a fucking eighth grader."

Okay. So I wasn't delusional. Here it was.

"Me, too," I said, more solemnly than I'd expected.

"I can't wait to see you," he said. "The thought makes me want to explode."

"Me, too," I said, my blood rushing through me like crashing tsunamis of hot liquid.

"It's weird, right?"

"Yeah. It is," I acknowledged of our barely nascent friendship. "I'd been conflicted but now . . . I'm just not. This is too amazing."

"I've been trying to wrap my brain around it but I can't."

"I've completely abandoned myself to it. I can't stop thinking about you," I gushed. The weird part was, I didn't even care about my candid verbal unleashing. "I don't want to stop thinking about you, either," I added, softly.

"Oh my god, you just made me hard," he said. The heat surged downward. "I'm walking on my deck fucking pitching a tent for you."

I felt a surge of heat jolt through my entire body. This is going to sound positively juvenile, but no one had ever really talked dirty to me on the phone! I felt a bolt sear m'down yonders. I felt blushed yet turned on, like the Church Chat lady who needed to pop in a Lifesaver and suck until the hole became big enough for the ring to fit on her finger.

"Finn, I have to kiss you," I whispered.

"It's all I think about," he whispered back.

It was too surreal. This was now officially past the point of no return. I knew it was wrong, but you only live once. His lips would be on me. Not on my locket. On my lips. I'd feel his tongue inside my mouth. And his arms around me. No matter what. And I couldn't fucking wait.

CHAPTER 21

*Wishing is good for us. Daydreams, fantasies,
castles in the air, and aspirations all drive us forward,
impel us to make things happen. They also tell us a lot
about ourselves. Our wishes come straight from our core.*

—Anonymous

FROM THAT POINT ON, WE SPOKE FOUR TIMES A DAY. AT
least. Between stolen convos were flurries of texts and even
one night, as I lay on my pillow, a bedtime tuck-in worthy of
a teenage fantasy.

"Sweet dreams, little witch," he said as I closed my eyes
in the dark room.

"I'll see you in them," I replied in an almost whisperlike
purrr. I never knew I could be this ballsy of a woman; it was
as if he'd ignited a sexy side I had never had the confidence
to explore. He elicited this tigress streak; I suddenly felt a
feline flirting take over my tone as the whisper escaped my
larynx. I felt that in my head I was carrying myself like the
woman I always wanted to be.

"I swear, I've seen you in mine many times," he confessed in a throaty whisper.

"Me, too."

"Two more days," he said, sighing.

"Thirty-six hours."

We said good night and I curled up under the down comforter in the basking bliss of something more magical than a crush. It did have a ring of the young to it—the physical innocence, for the time being at least, and the almost audible pitter-patter, the kind when you finish the slow song at the school dance and walk outside together, holding hands, hearts pounding. And after that first kiss, practically gliding. And like the youthful crushes that spear the heart and possess the mind, it was moving at a breakneck pace that I couldn't stop even if I wanted to. My every thought was consumed with Finn. Our mouths locked. I imagined what it would be like. Kissing the obsession of my adult life. What if it was totally vile and he tried to stick his tongue down my throat and lick my epiglottis? What if there was zero chemistry and I felt mouth-raped and icky? You know what? Good! Then I could go back to my life and move on and not sit and mull over this rock-star fantasy.

But truthfully, all these so-called worries about lack of sparks in person were all bullshit, and I knew it. I had felt a palpable frisson in the air just by his side, in the warehouse, at dinner, in the car, on the plane. Maybe there's no such thing as love at first sight, but this sure felt awfully close, despite the fact I was emotionally armed with reams of backstory in the press and his vivid soul-searing lyrics imprinted in my brain.

I passed out and heard Wylie come in around 1:00 A.M. but lay like spaghetti so as not to initiate a whole convo about my departure. I felt guilty that I didn't feel guilty. Was I a guy? I loved him, of course, but somehow Finn transcended our life and was this whole new dimension, almost like I could compartmentalize the two distinct emotions for two totally different men. I'd heard men were better than women at doing this, but at the moment, as I heard cute Wylie padding around and switching off the lights and climbing into bed, I knew I could give any dude a run for his money. I didn't know what I wanted—I guess to have my cake and eat it, too? Have a torrid affair with Finn and get him out of my system and come back to patient Wylie after that sexual itch has been scratched? Or was I even feeling these things because something with Wylie wasn't quite right? If Wylie was my true love, it wouldn't even be possible to be dreaming of Finn unbuttoning my blouse, right? My mind was reeling a mile a minute. Until it finally slowed and I fell fast asleep.

CHAPTER 22

All fantasy should have a solid base in reality.
—Max Beerbohm

MY LAST DAY AT WORK WAS A FLURRY OF PRETRIP PHONE
calls, putting out minifires, and then facilitating, greeting, touring the MTV camera crew that was shooting our office as Noah offered the network an exclusive sneak peek at Pimps N' Ho's V. So in the midst of a shitstorm of tasks, I had production assistants asking me where "the crapper be at" and where in the neighborhood they could find a Duane Reade, muttering something about a hangover.

"This is my little right hand, Hazel!" Noah said with a small squeeze to my shoulder for the camera as I awkwardly held up my hand, as if to say "Hi, Mom." I looked like I had been run over by the burrito truck on Bedford so was hoping I'd wind up on the cutting-room floor. I couldn't get a thing done I was so preoccupied by the onslaught of chaos from the visiting MTV News posse, and even more distracting was the inner cacophony of the separate voices—moral, passionate, impetuous, conservative—all talking over one another.

Finally the day ended and I walked out, leaving ten Post-its with where everything was, my numbers, my hotel, a stool sample. Kidding. But shockingly, as the mother hen it was like the place fell apart when I traveled. I came home and packed my bags and headed to Kira's. Drew was going to put the kids to bed so she could take me to the airport and spend a little time with me predeparture.

I arrived to find her with two of her friends, Meg and Serena, in their weekly Tots n' Tonic hangout, where mommies cracked the booze and the kids plopped on the floor with a pile of naked Barbies.

"Here she is!" Kira said as I came in.

I hugged her and kissed Meg and Serena, who I had also grown close to through the years.

"Oh my god, the kids are so BIG!" I exclaimed. I hadn't seen them since Iris's last birthday party five months ago. "You guys sprouted."

They looked at me like I was a total doof, like, "Yeah, bitch, it happens."

"God I feel so dumb and old saying that. Don't you remember when people said that to you and you were just like, okay, bye."

"Totally," said Meg. "Though they dig it. They're psyched to be older-looking. They think it'll help them get Lady Gaga tickets next tour. Lexi wouldn't speak to me for three days after Nick and I went without her."

"Oh my god these kids grow up so fast these days," I said, shaking my head.

"Ki, tell her what Iris said!"

"What?"

"Oh my god—Hazel, Iris comes in this morning and jumps on our bed and goes, 'I made up a joke!' so Drew says 'Okay, let 'er rip' and she says: 'What did the asshole say to the butt cheek?' "

"NO! Come on!" I laughed. "What *did* the asshole say to the butt cheek?"

"Hey, neighbor!"

"That's not bad." I giggled.

"Wait, Aunt Hazel, I have another!" she said, beaming with pride. "How do you wake up Lady Gaga?"

I looked at Kira, trying to hold in my laughter. "Uh, I don't know, Iris, how do you wake up Lady Gaga?"

"Poker face!"

"I'm so proud," Kira said, rolling her eyes.

Serena leaned in to me with a whisper and said, "Who cleans Lady Gaga's pool?"

"Uh . . . I don't know," I said.

"Alejandro!" she guffawed. "I made that one up."

I burst out laughing at the un-PCness of these über-moms, realizing round two of the Tots n' Tonic playdate was clearly kicking in.

"Okay girls, *andiamo*! I gotta take my little sis to her flight, but you guys stay as long as you want."

"Drew!" I said, going to give my brother-in-law a hug. "Ready for daddy-time?"

"Yeah, *Velveteen Rabbit*. I'm sitting there crying like a *b-i-t-c-h* reading this book."

"All right, have fun!"

We kissed everyone good-bye and bolted. I could tell Kira was so psyched to get out of the house and whiz down the street in her car.

"I love Meg," I said.

"You know she wipes herself only with Puffs Plus now, no toilet paper."

"WHAT?"

"Yeah. Puffs Plus. Boutique boxes. Charmin's too rough for her royal sphincter or something."

"Shut the fuck up."

"Swear!" she said, holding a hand off the wheel. "God, I'm just so happy to be OUT!" Kira shouted joyfully as the cold air from the open window blew back her blond hair. "I swear, I'm housebound! I'm Upper East Side–bound. I sometimes can't breathe with all the snobby people and homogeneous neighbors. I feel like I'm trapped sometimes. I'm so jealous of you right now."

"Kira, you know every girl in New York would kill for your life, don't you? Gorgeous children, gorgeous apartment, gorgeous husband . . ."

"I know. I'm so lucky. I know I am, and yet I would give anything to be getting on a plane to L.A. right now. Not even to go make out with Finn fucking Schiller, just to fly off to the sun and have an adventure. The older you get, the narrower the sieve gets that your life pours you down. So you're going to go and live it all for both of us."

I looked out the window, getting chills as I thought about it. I looked back at my sister.

"Kira, this is our secret. I'm not telling a soul. Wylie and I are taking a break and I just . . . need to do this."

"To the grave," my sister said, in all seriousness.

"This is all so surreal," I said. "I can't believe he's picking me up. Well, I guess his driver is, too, so not, like baggage claim PDA or anything, but I feel like I'm going to explode."

"Listen, Hazel. I've been thinking about this nonstop. Every single second. I love Drew, I really do. I adore him. But you know life doesn't have to be so black and white. I know you love Wylie, but this is something outside of you guys—"

"I think the same thing, but I don't think he's seeing it that way."

"I just feel like you need to go there and fucking live your life. Do it for me, at the very least, I'll be sitting here dying!" she gushed. "You just don't want to blink and have all the exciting parts of your life over and wish you had acted on this. Trust me, it becomes 'too late' too soon. The second I came home with my baby and was up all night I knew it was the beginning of her story and it wasn't about me anymore. My needs went out the window, and I want you to do as much as you can, pack it all in before you decide—if you decide—to settle down. Because it really is 'settling' in a way. You settle for letting go of that piece of yourself that fantasizes about what life has in store for you. And you begin to think about what it has in store for someone else. Your child."

I swallowed the lump in my throat. "That's so fucking depressing," I said.

"Look, I love my life, LOVE my girls and Drew. I'm just saying there's a monotony that I don't want for you, unless you sign up one hundred percent sure that's what you want. Not just because people do it or I did it. I would never want you to march along without at least daring to shake it up a little." I saw a little glint in my sister's eye.

"Are you telling me to fuck Finn?" I teased.

She smiled. "I'm telling you to carpe the fucking diem."

"Here we are, American," I said, pointing to my terminal.

We pulled up and she gave me a long hug. I felt so lucky to have a safe, nonjudgmental friend in her; all my other pals would shit over this.

"I love you, Hazel."

"Love you, Kira," I said. "Thank you."

CHAPTER 23

All the works of man have their origin in creative fantasy.
What right have we then to depreciate imagination.
—Carl Gustav Jung

I HAD PASSED OUT ON THE PLANE, IN A SLUMBER MIRRORING
an autopsy patient on the slab. I was so deep under that
I didn't even put my seat back, so no one woke me to put
it back. I reentered the world of the living literally as the
wheels hit the runway at LAX. Shocked, I immediately went
for my little makeup kit and tossed my hair up into what
Kira and I always called a Bamm-Bamm ponytail but was
actually Pebbles, high and bunlike. I put on some powder to
absorb the oil spill on my face that rivaled British Petroleum,
and some lipstick. But then I imagined our Robert Doisneau–
style kiss and rethought that. I wiped it off. I didn't want him
to kiss me and then have smeared twisted-clownlike mouth
and look like Heath Ledger's Joker. Okay, a little Rosebud
Salve and a spritz of perfume. Okay, Hazel. Breathe.

I walked off the jetway, headed toward the departure/
drop-off area, where Finn said he'd meet me. My head darted

around in every direction as the onslaught of traveling hordes coursed in all directions. I felt like an animal in the woods knowing the hunter was there. But instead of bullets spraying my dead ass, it was Cupid's gold-tipped arrow headed for my bum. I stopped dead in my racks next to Mex in the City cantina and made eye contact. Both of us grinned huge shiteaters and picked up our paces as we approached each other. Personally, I would've jogged into full dash but tried to play it slightly cooler than the Bulgarians who tore their hair out screaming for Michael Jackson in the late 1980s.

"Hazel," he simply said, reaching for my face.

His ice blue eyes flickered with warmth as he smiled and leaned in, his lips electrifying mine. I threw my arms around him, and we dissolved into each other in an embrace so fierce and blinding, it was as if all the Tumi-draggers around us faded into blurred props, cardboard cutouts, set dressing in the drama that starred this very liplock. A very public kiss that somehow made the rest of the world stop, as if we were shrouded in our own red velvet love nest and not the buzzing concourse of an international airport. His mouth was hot and wet and delicious. Honey? Citrus? His hands touched my neck then my shoulders, and finally, gasping, we parted and looked at each other.

"You take my breath away," he said.

"Me, too," I said, practically panting. "I mean literally, I'm hyperventilating."

Flush and glowing, we both walked hand in hand to the exit, Finn relieving me of my bag as we headed to his car. One or two young people did double takes noticing us, but in general even a rock band of The Void's stature would go unnoticed by the neck-pillow-carrying masses. We exited the building and headed toward his car. I had expected Sly to be there, but Finn had driven by himself.

"Awww, the rock star came and fetched me all by his lonesome?" I smiled, cocking my head to one side, like those children in Sears Portrait Studio.

"Yeah, we can do some things for ourselves. I just started brushing my own teeth, actually, and it's nice."

We got in the car and looked at each other.

Instant mauling.

I don't know if it was me or him or both but we dove toward each other, kissing like mad, until several honks summoned us to reality and the guard, who had been cool with letting the musician bend the rules to park there, rapped on the window as a gentle reminder to move the fuck on now that his ho'd been collected.

As we drove toward my hotel, I leaned over and kissed his cheek the entire way, dotting the bone with tiny almost inaudible pecks all the way down to his neck.

"Oh my god, those kisses . . . ," he said, focusing on the road.

I made my way back up to his ear and heard his breath quicken. I had no idea where this sex kitten thing came from, but I knew, he being who he was, that the rotating groupie assembly line at the Barbie factory obviously shagged him rotten, so something ignited a passion in me that was like nothing I had ever been seized with. Maybe I was a Mattel factory reject that came out with black hair and pale skin, but like the upside-down airplane stamp, I was hoping that would prove valuable to him.

"Oh my god, you're driving me crazy," he said.

Maybe better to calm down, I thought. It's not like I was going to blow him in the driver's seat. (But the thought had crossed my mind.) What had come over me?

I sat back in my seat, and he took my hand and kissed it.

"How was the trip?" he asked.

"I don't even remember. It was as if I crashed in a field of poppies like Dorothy. I was out. I think I've been kind of sleep deprived." I shrugged.

"Me, too," he said. "A lot of thinking about my little witch's visit."

I had chills. He squeezed my hand. "How was the visit with your nieces?"

"Great, they're so cute. So precocious," I said, shaking my head. I told him Iris's joke, and he almost crashed he was laughing so hard.

"I bet you were a little spitfire," he said.

"I was, I definitely was," I admitted. "But I wasn't as advanced with the language as they are. But I was mischievous."

"Like how?" he asked.

"Not like, lighting shit on fire or anything, I just had some serious 'tude. My report cards always had high marks for academics but they checked poor for behavior. I was restless. Especially in stupid stuff, like gym," I said, smiling. "Once my phys ed teacher screamed at me and said, 'MISS LAVERY! THERE IS NO *I* IN *TEAM*!' I calmly looked at her and replied, 'Yes, but there is an *M* and an *E*.'"

"Brilliant." He laughed. "Wait, why doesn't everyone realize that?" he asked, confounded.

"I honestly don't know! That's why that expression has always driven me fucking nuts."

"*You* drive me nuts," he said, patting my leg. "You're fucking adorable."

I felt a surge of heat rush through my chest. "Wait, what are we doing?" I asked.

"I'm pulling over. It's been way too long since I've kissed you."

We pulled into a burger shack parking lot and Finn put his hand on my cheek and pulled me toward him. We kissed and kissed, making out like a couple of teenagers. It was just us, a boy and a girl, so perfectly simple, and simply perfect.

He pulled back and looked at me. "That kiss of yours."

"Yours," I said. "Ours?"

He paused, exhaling, looking at his lap. I took his hand in mine.

"And what about the boyfriend?" he asked.

Wylie. Gulp. My heart felt a momentary ache. But my head trumped it and sent in the mental broom and dustpan to quickly swoop in and sweep away the dust bunnies of guilt that floated in at the sound of his name. I exhaled my vision of our apartment and the smells of the meal he'd labored over.

"I care about Wylie, I do, Finn. But . . . you are something entirely new to me, and I need to explore it. This is the most alive I've felt. I know I just met you and I know this makes zero sense, but I've never felt anything this intense before."

"Me neither. Ever."

We looked at each other and then my eyes darted to the clock.

"What time is your first meeting?" he asked.

"Soon. But I'm fine. I don't even need to unpack, I'll just chuck my shit at the front desk, and Clarissa, the local PR and events girl here, is picking me up downstairs."

"Well, I get you tonight, so I suppose I can spare you for your work," he said as I reached my arm around him and leaned in to kiss his temple as he pulled the car out and got back onto the road.

"How is the album coming?" I asked.

"Fits and starts," he added. "Though since I met you I got a few ideas," he said.

Moi? Inspiring Finn Schiller? I thought I would swoon and smash into the air bag compartment.

"I just have so many interruptions because of the tour coming up in Europe," he added. "I leave in two weeks."

"Oh, is it that soon?" I asked, trying to sound nonchalant. The thought of him leaving made me nauseated, even though we lived in different cities anyway.

"But it's a short leg, two months."

I felt ill. "Oh, great," I managed to sputter out.

"I always write tons of songs on the road and then afterward I just crash for a week or two. I'm fine on time though, so I'm not worried. I just had a little block for the last few months and somehow you triggered the flow to return, so thank you. You've quickly become my muse, Hazel."

"You're welcome," I said, cheerfully. "Should I go get a toga and eat grapes and stuff now?"

"You can, actually. There's a great bespoke toga haberdashery on Melrose, I hear."

So we pulled up to my hotel and I was gripped by an acute pain at leaving Finn's side for even a few hours.

"Have a great day, Hazel."

"You, too, thank you so much for the special VIP scooping up from LAX. No one in New York does that."

"I wouldn't let my inspiration take a taxi," he said, motioning for me to come closer. We kissed softy and I swear I had chills through my entire body.

"What?" he asked, reading my out-of-it face.

"Nothing, that just—" I gathered my breath. "That just gave me such warm fuzzies. I feel like a Muppet or something."

"Well, I can't wait to unzip your Grover suit later, then," he said.

I smiled and blew him a kiss through the window. He mimed catching it, then smacked it on his face as he pulled out, waving good-bye.

CHAPTER 24

Ambition is not what a man would do, but what a man does,
for ambition without action is fantasy.
—Bryant H. McGill

THE ATTEMPT TO WORK WAS PURE FOLLY. THERE WAS NO
effing way I could possibly focus, so I sloshed through my
day, nodding at information about alcohol sponsors and VIPs
and schwag bags for certain celebs, their handlers, stylists,
and Svengalis who had promised their asses would be there.

"Sure," I said blithely. "Just tell me what you need, you
got it."

I kept stealing glances at my watch. We went to Finn's
space and did a quote unquote "walk through" with the full
team, which weirdly included north of twenty people. My
eyes were practically glazing over after the discussions of
which hue enormous Chinese lanterns were being used,
and the lighting designer was arguing with the floral con-
cept person, and both kept looking at me for cues.

"Huh?" I asked, snapping back to the moment.

"Which do you prefer, the bright red or the orange?"

"Oh, uh . . ." Finn had a bright orange stripe across his all-black CD two albums ago. "Orange."

Next we spoke with the caterers, who clearly didn't understand that the joystick-whacking heathens who were coming to this did not want to hear the words "aioli drizzle."

"Look, not to insult your chef's creative talents or anything, but we just want sliders. Satays. No criss-cut potato galettes please, these are gamers," I tried to say delicately. But truthfully I just wanted to get the fuck out.

FINALLY after four hours of round-robin meetings with the various vendors, Clarissa drove me back to the hotel, where I filled a huge bubble bath and soaked. I soaked in my options and my life and just wanted the lather to wash away all the guilt, all the question marks. The problem was I truly didn't know what I wanted out of life. But what I did know was that this moment was the single most exhilarating, exciting thing that had ever happened to me. I felt like I could fly. Not in the R. Kelly cheezoid way but just free, like after trudging through the last years I finally had wings. No Red Bull needed.

CHAPTER 25

I think one of the best guides to telling you who you are,
and I think children use it all the time for this purpose,
is fantasy.
—Peter Shaffer

"YOU LOOK ABSOLUTELY GORGEOUS," FINN SAID AS I CAME
outside.

I blushed as the doorman helped me inside and I kissed
Finn hello.

"I know you told me you've been dating a chef, so I can't
compete with that. But I do have something up my sleeve,"
he said.

"Honestly, I could eat an S.O.S. pad right now and it
would be a five-star dish," I said. "I don't even care. I don't
need to eat."

He started driving as I recounted the chaos of my day,
and I saw we were approaching unfamiliar territory.

"Where are we going?" I asked excitedly.

"Remember you told me you cried when John Hughes
died?"

"Yes, I'm still not over it," I said.

"I took a page from one of your movies."

"What, you're bringing me to a rich kids party where everyone's named like Blaine or Shayne?"

"No." He laughed. "You'll see."

We approached the looming space-age whiteness of the Getty.

"I can't paint for shit but thought you'd like this."

He pulled in and stopped the car.

"Wait a minute," I said, eyes widening. "Are you kidding me? Are we going into the Getty?"

"A friend of a friend pulled some strings."

We went inside and were greeted by Finn's acquaintance, who thanked him profusely for the signed T-shirts and concert tickets.

"I'm the one who needs to thank you," Finn said, shaking his hand gratefully. "This is spectacular."

"Right this way," the guy said.

We followed him down the hallways and into an all-glass room with a small table lit with hurricane lamps and covered in flowers and wineglasses.

"Oh my god, Finn . . . ," I said, eyes about to water. "I always wanted to be Amanda Jones!" I could not fucking believe this was happening. Kira would keel.

An attractive server came out, offering me choices a caterer had prepared in the back, and afterward I sipped my incredible red wine and reached over and took Finn's hand.

"I can't get over this. Never in my whole life," I said, shaking my head. "I am going to wake up now and it's going to suck."

Finn stood up, holding my hand, leading me across the room. "You can take the wine. Let's walk around."

I met his gaze, and he leaned in and kissed me.

"Oh, and Hazel, you're not dreaming."

We wandered the halls, sticking our noses in such treasures as Leonardo da Vinci's sketchbook, Dürer and Altdorfer etchings, and Sisley landscapes. I was pinching myself with every step.

"So who's that guy? Don't tell me his dad's the janitor and you met in detention . . . ," I joked.

"No, he's one of the curators for the museum. One of the trustees is a fan and pulled some strings."

Strings? More like steel cables. I simply was in shock.

We walked back hand in hand and ate our dinner. I was so nervous, not quite knowing how to broach the subject of your place or mine, but as it turned out, I didn't have to.

"Let's walk outside in the garden," he said as I relished the final bites of the espresso gelato we'd been served for dessert.

My pulse pounded as I took his hand and followed him down a winding path with a steep pitch under the most stunning of yellow moons.

"I have a question," I ventured, figuring there's no point in playing games. "How many girls have you brought here?"

He stopped and looked at me, as if insulted. "None."

I laced my arm around his. "I didn't mean to imply there was a revolving door of women here or anything, but you have to admit this is a total snow job."

"I don't think many of the women I've hung out with would even care about this."

"Trust me, they would. This is amazing."

"It's amazing to you, but many girls just think it's amazing to be in a hotel suite with a band. They wouldn't care about art. They think Getty is just a gas station."

"That whole *Almost Famous* 'I'm with the band' thing is so not me."

"I know. I can tell," he said, stopping and facing me. I still couldn't get over the surreal vision of staring at Finn's face. In the moonlight, no less. In a private garden sequestered from the world, the chorus of fans' cries, or gasps of passersby noticing their cult-worshipped idol on the street.

Finn delicately took my face in his hands and kissed me so tenderly and so perfectly I literally felt a charge surge through my body, like I'd been plugged in when our mouths met. My fuse lit with a glowing, blindingly intense light from within as my tongue searched his and I melted into him. I put my hands in his hair and let my finger trace a line down the back of his neck, feeling a tiny mole. I smiled, turning him around to see it, but he was too tall.

"Bend down a little," I said. He did, and I kissed the sweet dot as I felt him shiver.

He exhaled, turned back, and grabbed me, lifting me off the ground and kissing me as he held me in his arms, my legs wrapped around him. I didn't even know I could be lifted off the ground like a flying weightless cheerleader, but it felt amazing.

"Wait, Finn, are there cameras and stuff out here?" I asked, looking for hidden lenses perched in the foliage.

He looked up and around then spied a little cove of trees and shrubs and led me across the path to the other side's Eden of green grass, flowers, and manicured hedges. It was like our own verdant cave, impenetrable and cozy. He sat down in the grass and pulled me down to him as I laughed at the insanity of the moment, lying on him and kissing his neck and collarbone as I felt his hands slide up the back of my shirt. His skin on mine felt incredible. He somehow snapped off my bra one-handed and moved his hands up my entire back, with such a passion and force it was as if I were clay and he was sculpting me into a Venus. Which is what I felt like—a total goddess. I felt him hard beneath me, and he broke our kiss and looked up at me.

"God you're beautiful, Hazel."

"You are." I didn't know what else to say. He was.

"From the moment I saw you," he said, "I thought you were stunning."

What? "Let's not go that far."

"Why? You are."

He pulled me back down to him, and I lay beside him, kissing in the grass for what seemed like hours as we grew more heated and breathless. Finally I pulled his shirt off and we both sighed when our chests touched and our arms could fully envelop the other in a naked embrace.

"You feel amazing," he said. "Your skin . . ."

"Finn," I said in a lusty tone I'd never heard escape my mouth. "I want you."

He looked at me with a flash in his eyes as he grabbed me and kissed my breast, cupping the other in his hand. I was so turned on it was like all my fantasies rolled into this colossal moment. He reached down and unbuttoned his black jeans and reached up my skirt, yanking off my lace panties. He reached into his pocket and retrieved some sort of sheep condom and unrolled it, looking at me the entire time. Okay good, no awkward convo about my contracting hepatitis F from some backstage roadwhore. Our eyes were locked in the almost kaleidoscopic magic of our shared beat in time, and he pressed into me as I gasped out loud. He moved so slowly and so sweetly, kissing me with each tender push deeper, that I truly thought I would come right then and there.

"Finn," I whispered as he kissed my neck.

"Hazel, you feel fucking amazing."

I looked up at the sky behind him, the glittering yellow

diamond moon, the flowers whose vibrant hues I could still make out in the darkness, the botanical bliss of mingling fragrances, the faint chirp of muted crickets. And the taste of Finn's mouth. It was such a feast for all the senses, but touch. My god, I'd never fucked like this. The sheer ecstasy of Finn being inside me, moving just how I would have directed, made me arch my back in absolute abandon. He started to move faster as I somehow allowed a louder moan to escape my lungs, but before embarrassment could surge I realized he met mine with his own.

"Oh god, Hazel."

We moved in the most perfect rhythm of each other's wild embrace in some kind of fused holy shared song of breath and wind-blown leaves.

"Finn . . ."

"I'm close, Hazel. You feel so incredible."

"I'm close, too—" Normally I would close my eyes as I felt the intensity spike and my nerves screaming, but I forced myself to keep them open. I looked at him and the almost glittering setting, as if we were seeing the world with a black light and each color—his blue eyes, the yellow moon, the pink posies—glowed with the phosphorescent glint of a color wheel on acid.

He moved faster, deeper, gripping back with his hand beneath me, and I heard my name grow from a whisper to a panting echo.

"Hazel," he said. "Hazel—"

"Oh my god," I said, feeling the surge approaching. "Finn—"

"Hazel—" He then grew silent and thrust into me so deep my eyes closed as my whole body racked with an ecstasy I had never known.

He looked at me, glistening and spent. "I don't think I've

ever come so hard. Not since I was fucking seventeen, at least," he said. Somehow when he talked a little dirtily it revved me up even more. I was so flattered, despite not fully believing him.

"Me neither," I admitted, truthfully. Wylie and I happened to have a killer sex life, but I always wanted to do adventurous things, like outdoors or at people's parties, and he was always loath to try it. Wylie loved making love and always took care of my needs, but somehow it almost felt hotter to have someone use me for pleasure instead of worrying about me the whole time. And here I was, the first time with Finn, and it was 100 percent pure risk, a whole new dimension, as if someone had taken the box off sex— no bed, no ceiling even, just sheets of green soft grass and under a cloak of stars. Real stars.

I paused for a moment, thinking of Wylie's plastic glow-in-the-dark ones he'd fashioned into such a sweet proposal, but the thought shot away like a stellar implosion, soaring and burning away in a flicker against the cobalt sky. I blinked.

Finn leaned his head on my chest as I put my hands through his hair, staring above at the constellations.

"I can't even speak," I said. "That was like . . . religious."

"I know what you mean," he said. "I could die here and just be beamed right to St. Peter a happy man."

"You know I tried to keep my eyes open but you felt so good they somehow kept closing so I could focus on the rush," I explained. "But even still, I can't get over the view and your face and just . . . the sheer perfection of this. I'm . . . smitten."

"I'm smitten, Hazel," he said, leaning up on his strong muscular arm next to me. He took his finger and traced a heart on my heart.

I started feeling some dripping action below and looked around for my bag, retrieving some pocket Kleenex.

"By the way, I'm on the pill, so don't worry. I'm not gonna, like, hijack your sperm or anything."

"Oh good, 'cause that's exactly what I was just worrying about," he said sarcastically. "What are you, crazy?"

"No, I'm serious! Trust me, there are tons of women here who would love to have a rock star as their baby daddy."

"Since when are you like tons of women?"

"I'm not, but I just wanted you to know I'm not trying to like, harvest some seed."

"Oh, good," he joked. "Phew."

"So, um, do rock stars cuddle? Or is that not cool?"

He smiled and took me in his arms. "Who says it's not cool?"

"Well, I just don't associate exploding guitar riffs and sexy growls with, ya know, spooning."

"You better start," he said, wrapping his arms around me.

CHAPTER 26

I never let a fantasy get away,
because I always stop to analyze it.
—Shelley Duvall

DRESSED AND DEWY WE WALKED BACK TO THE CAR AS THE evening chill started to creep over us. I caught sight of myself in the window as he unlocked the passenger side, and I could have sworn I had little hearts jostling in my eyeballs like some Looney Tunes cast member. Except not a skunk. I was all woman in that moment; I felt more seductive, more sensual, more alive than I ever had. I sat in the car and watched Finn walk around to his side, and that was almost too long to go without touching him. He dove in and kissed me again, and we couldn't stop. Finally we parted lips and he looked at me, his brow raised.

"Fuck the hotel, come to my house?" he said, almost imploring me. "I want to have a sleepover."

I laughed. "I'm picturing my Iris and her friends in their

Mini Boden pajamas and SpongeBob sleeping bags," I said. "But, okay. Only if you have Paul Newman's popcorn."

"I think we can rustle some up," he said, winking as we drove. The lights of Los Angeles melted into neon streams as my eyes viewed the world as if intoxicated. I'd only had a glass or two of wine, but I felt as if I were drugged on the narcotic of Finn's embrace, the hallucinatory nature of my experience difficult to reconcile with reality as the car sped higher into the hills and his hand seemed to squeeze mine harder with each hairpin turn upward.

"Here we are," he said, pulling into the most magnificent house. It was the definition of my taste—creepy almost, old Hollywood, but understated without the douche bag grandeur one might've imagined. This wasn't *Entourage*, it was pure Finn Schiller, just what I would have pictured for him. He walked around and took my hand, helping me out as we walked up to the ivy-covered exterior, where he punched in a long code and the door opened.

Inside, a modern interior accented with some antique mahogany pieces of furniture lent a cool air to an already impressive domicile. Finn crossed the room and opened a bottle of whiskey and uncorked a red wine for me and led me upstairs. His room was overlooking the whole city with a deck outside. I sipped my wine, and he put his drink down on the ledge and kissed me. I tasted the whiskey in his mouth, and it turned me on even more as we made out like teens outside among the glittering lights below. We staggered back to his enormous ebony four-poster bed fit for a king, or at least *Billboard* chart-topper, and fell onto it, rolling over each other in a delicious mélange of fevered breaths broken by smiles and kisses. We made love again, and this time, even though it was just in a bed like everyone else, it possessed all the magic of our splendor in the grass, it could have been the moon hanging above us versus the canopy, and it felt just the same. I arched my back as I felt him inside me, as a climax beckoned in the distance.

"Don't stop," I begged.

"Hazel . . ." He felt so wildly amazing I couldn't believe this was real, and we finally both collapsed into the tightest full-body hug I've ever known. I looked at his face and I felt tears well up.

"Are you okay, sweet girl?" he asked, a look of concern flashing across his brow.

"Yes, yes," I assured him. "I'm just so happy."

I hope that didn't freak him out, but it was true. It was a feeling of euphoria I couldn't have fathomed possible.

"Me, too," he replied, touching my hair. "I'm crazy about you."

"Me, too. Just smitten," I said, leaning in to kiss him.

He put his arm around me and tapped his shoulder. "Put your head here," he instructed as I happily obliged.

"You know, I never ever can sleep intertwined with someone, but in this moment, I feel like I could pass out," I confessed.

"Really? You never sleep tangled up?" he marveled. I was surprised by his reaction, given the probable scores of girls he's bedded, and I hardly envisioned someone snuggling with a one-nighter.

"No, I love a cuddle, but then I like to roll over and have my own space. But not now—" I quickly added. "I like it here, on you."

I felt a beat of sadness recalling my morning Velcro-fests with Wylie, the only man I'd ever really loved to cuddle.

"Well, good sweet girl," he said, kissing my forehead

tenderly. "You have a big day tomorrow. Sleep as long as you can."

My eyelids grew heavy until somewhere, for the first time in my life, I drifted off sleeping in someone's arms. The arms of Finn Schiller, no less. My last conscious image against the movie screens of my closed eyelids was his face.

CHAPTER 27

Dreams are not without meaning
wherever they may come from—from fantasy,
from the elements, or from other inspiration.
—Paracelsus

"WHERE ARE YOU?" CLARISSA BARKED. "I'M IN THE LOBBY OF
your hotel and buzzed up three times!"

"Oh, uh—I fucked up. I'm at the hair place. Meet me at
the event space in an hour."

"Okay," she said, sounding not okay, but since I was
paying her, she was sucking it up.

"Sorry—see you in a bit."

I put my phone back in the jacket pocket I'd fumbled
toward on the floor and found myself naked, looking at the
vast blue skies outside Finn's room. I looked around and
pieced together my passion-strewn wardrobe, finally discovering my other heel behind enormous drapes that flanked
the picture windows. I went into the coffee-colored marble
bathroom (noticing the extreme shower with six nozzles on

either side and a huge elephant-style head on top), borrowed some mouthwash and a hairbrush, and walked downstairs.

Finn was dressed at the table with a feast prepared by Sly, who greeted me with a nod.

"Hazel, do you like chocolate chips in your pancakes?" Finn asked as he poured a second glass of orange juice.

"Um, yeah! Who doesn't?"

I sat down and wasn't sure how to be in front of Sly. But before I could even open my mouth to interact, Finn leaned in and gave me a kiss. All my nerves of potential awkwardness subsided, and I felt so close to him. He reached across the table and took my hand in his and squeezed it, and I swear in doing so he scavenged several heartbeats. I was obsessed.

"I have to go down to the space for some press and the load-in," I said, wishing I could just stay there with him all day. "Is there any way I could call a cab?"

"Absolutely not, I'm taking you," Finn said.

"No, no, no—it's across town," I said, gesturing to the distant skyline of downtown L.A.

"I'd love it. It's close to my meeting anyway," he said.

We finished breakfast, and Sly cleared our plates with a knowing look and even a small smile in my direction as Finn took my hand, kissed it, and led me out to the garage. I was stunned to find six cars—all black—lined up. He picked the Aston Martin, and we hopped in.

"Oooh, this is so James Bondian," I swooned. "I'm really not a hot cars girl, I live in New York, but I know a fabulous one when I see it," I said.

He leaned in and kissed me as we pulled away from the house, which was even more stunning in the sunlight. He put on the radio, and I was elated to hear The The blaring, one of my favorites.

"Fuck, I'm so behind on the next record," he lamented. "I used to get so much writing done on the tours. Now it's just impossible."

"You don't write on the road anymore?"

"No. You know, the bigger the tours got, the more people surrounding me kissing my ass . . . it's hard to dig deep and get gritty when there are all these fucking sycophants. Last time I got shit done and it wasn't until I came home and decompressed that I could do a thing. I was in an old decaying synagogue where we set up a makeshift studio and really stripped it all down."

"I read you'd recorded in a funeral home, too—"

"Yeah, that was a really dark album. I was so out of it with drugs and just so down on the world. People. Relationships were dissolving around me, and I was just so disenchanted with fucking everyone."

"When did that spell end?" I probed.

"It hadn't . . . I mean, on and off, sure, but, not really until I met you. The morning of our flight I was in a fucking shittyass mood and tore Steve a new asshole for overscheduling me with bullshit shows I swore I'd never do, and just, felt so depressed."

"You've gone through so much, Finn. Have you ever tried a shrink? It might help—"

"I did. I tried. Cocksucker wanted to dig so deep into my childhood and asked a trillion questions about infancy and all this crap. I was just like, dude, fucking make me feel better NOW. My head was splitting from pain. I never dealt with lots of grief I had, and I just thought I was a grenade ready to be tossed."

". . . you pulled the pin on my grenade of a life," I sang, from his song "Thrown."

"You got it." He put his hand on my leg and looked at

me. I looked at his worn hand on the steering wheel, his leather sleeve covering his wrist. He was so sexy I couldn't stand it. He embodied the intoxicating blend of toughness with such an emotional undercurrent.

"It was a rough, miserable time," he continued. "But look, I got my best work out of it."

We swerved across two lanes to the exit and headed down the street into the downtown area and pulled up to the space, where already huge trucks blocked off the street. Clarissa had secured all the permits for us, and the lighting people, caterers, and music folk were all already unloading into the raw space.

"Full-scale operation you have cooking here." Finn smiled, observing the chaos.

"Yup. I don't mess around!"

"Come here, precious girl."

I leaned in and kissed him before zipping out to face the whirlwind of prebash chaos.

"See you at eightish?" I asked.

"I can't wait, little witch."

CHAPTER 28

Fantasy allows you to bend the world and the situation to more clearly focus on the moral aspects of what's happening. In fantasy you can distill life down to the essence of your story.
—Terry Goodkind

IT WAS TIME. I'D RUN AROUND LIKE A DECAPITATED CHICKEN for four hours, overseeing Clarissa's staff of cuties with headsets and clipboards and six-inch stilettos with fuck-me red bottoms. The dimmers were set, the music began to fill the cavernous space. The dark purple gels glowed through the loft, and as the base boomed, gorgeous male-model cater-waiters began offering hors d'oeuvres to the early guests, who were mostly staffers from my office.

"Holy shit, Hazel, you BROUGHT IT!" my coworker Christopher screamed from across the massive dance floor. John gave me a thumbs-up by the bar as he chatted up a peroxided nincompoop, and I spied Noah drinking it all in. Shots included.

Noah hung up his cell as I walk toward him and Sergei, who raised a glass of purple Pimp's Punch in my direction.

"My god, girl," Noah marveled, engulfing me in a bear hug. "Promotion. Raise. Whatever you want, Hazel, this is SICK," he said, looking up at the dizzying collage of colored strobes. "Hey, where were you?"

"Oh, I was changing in the back. I stashed my party dress and heels in my bag. Didn't think you wanted me to show up in the jeans-and-bun look I've been sporting this afternoon."

"So, Haze, he'll be there? Our landlord for the evening?" Noah asked, eyes ablaze.

"Yup. Just texted with him."

"You text with Finn Schiller?" Christopher asked. "Get out."

I had, in fact, just texted with him. He said he missed me. Kira asked me to send pics, so I'd walked around snapping away, e-mailing her a little photo essay of "before" photos.

In minutes it would be after.

A flurry of guests checked their cars at the valet, passed my gaggle of name checkers, and brushed by velvet rope–opening huge security guards and made for one of the four bars.

"So many hot chicks here," Noah drooled. "This place is a total smokeshow!"

I tried not to gloat. I knew that my boss truly just wanted a hot crowd and tons of press. Check and check. The place was packed within the first forty-five minutes, but all I could do was crane my neck for Finn.

I was walking Noah through an interview line with *Extra* when I felt arms around me.

I had been behind the camera, watching the bimbo in-terviewer ask Noah about his "vision" for the game and the world he was creating, when Finn's serpentine arms wrapped their way around my waist as I shivered. The leather pushed through the thin material of my dress, and I was instantly electrified. I kept focus on Noah, who was happily chatting away as Finn's lips dotted the back of my neck.

Suddenly there was a lull in the rapid-fire Q & A fest that had been bantering in the background. Noah's jaw was practically on the floor looking at us.

"Uh—"

"So it's an edgier, darker world this time?" the girl asked as Noah tried to snap back into focus.

"Yeah, yeah, it's the underbelly, really, what lingers in the shadows of this milieu . . ."

I had taken Finn's hand and led him away and could almost feel Noah's neck stretching, like something out of *Beetlejuice*, to see where we were going. We charged through the crowds, past the dancers on blocks, past the bartenders, through to the back, beyond the kitchen, and into a back area where I'd stashed all my stuff.

Against the dirty windows he pressed himself against me, the same locale where we'd first cooked up the air between us with chaste exchanges. But this time we could have steamed up all the glass in the warehouse with those kisses. The throbbing bass from the DJ muted, as if we were making out underwater, isolated in our own ecosystem of raging desire uncorked from the memory of our previous encounter.

"How much longer do you have to stay?" he asked, looking at his vintage tank watch.

"Zero minutes," I said. I'd delivered. I knew I was golden and could parachute out.

We took off, speeding down the hills and onto Sunset as

I turned from my window back to Finn. He was so beautiful it almost hurt to look at him. I was so thoroughly exhilarated I felt tipsy. Then, before I could even think straight, I blurted the unthinkable.

"Finn . . ."

"Yes, sweet girl—"

"Finn, this is crazy. I am so wild about you, this has to be more than some kind of infatuation."

He looked at me, his ice blue eyes misty. "I know, I feel the same way."

"Yeah?"

"Hazel, I was actually thinking . . . will you come on my tour with me? To Europe?"

Um . . . that was better than any invitation I'd ever gotten. "Really?" I beamed.

"Really. I'd love it."

"Okay . . . yes!"

I lunged across the console and threw my arms around him and kissed the whole side of his face nonstop as he laughed.

He pulled over to the side of the road and we could not stop kissing. I ran my hands through his hair and when we finally broke apart his smile matched mine and I thought I would die of happiness. We held hands the rest of the trip, and when we pulled into his driveway, I reached for the door handle and he stopped me, grabbing me and practically throwing me into the backseat. He took my hand and put it on his jeans, so I could feel how hard he was, which ignited a thousand wicks inside my body. Our collective mercury would've lit the Tylenol alarms as our scalding bodies found each other and we sighed as our skin met again. His ardor turned me on even more as he gently turned me over and took me from behind. I was lying on his backseat as my hands reached up the door as he pushed inside me. I screamed as he moved from slower to fast and slow again, as I took him in and literally started to see stars. His hands held my waist, then my breasts, then stroked my back as I heard my name grow from a whisper to a yelled HAZEL as he collapsed on top of me. When I felt him I shivered into a full-body climax that shook my core and made me dizzy.

"Babe, that was incredible," he said.

I felt him squeeze me as the side of his face rested on my back. I closed my eyes and savored the bliss of that heap of spent limbs and the echo of each other's names in the night air.

I turned around and he grabbed me so hard I thought he'd wring the very oxygen from my lungs and we gripped each other as if we could never let go.

After our pants slowed to regular inhalations, we kissed once more.

He looked at me and moved the hair from my face as he gently put a hand on each of my cheeks. "Let's go make some popcorn."

CHAPTER 29

The human soul has still greater need of the ideal
than the real. It is by the real that we exist and
by the ideal that we live.
—Victor Hugo

I AWOKE THE NEXT MORNING AND LAY THERE STARING AT him, pinching myself and also wondering if he really meant it about the tour. How did I follow up? What if we wound up together? Would I wind up living here with him, being Mrs. Finn Schiller? Would I have little rock star babies who traveled on a tour bus? Okay, Hazel . . . you're getting ahead of yourself. God, we'd have cute kids. And every name goes with Schiller practically. He must be ready, I mean, he was in his forties!

His eyes opened. He reached over and leaned in to kiss me.

"Wait—don't—" I stammered.

"Why?"

"I have a really bad case of the zacklies," I confessed sheepishly.

"What are the zacklies?" he asked.

"I haven't brushed my teeth yet. It's when your breath smells zackly like your ass."

He laughed. "I don't care."

"No, I do. This is still too new. I have to go Scopeify."

I ran to the bathroom and chugged some mouthwash and came back to find him crunching a wint-o-green Lifesaver.

"Those glow in the dark, you know."

"They do not."

"Yeah, if you crunch it in the dark, there's green sparky things."

"Bullshit."

I took his hand and led him naked into his enormous walk-in closet lined with identical leather jackets and black jeans.

I closed the door behind us so it was pitch-black and stood him in front of the full-length mirror.

"Okay, chew."

He crunched away, and sure enough, bright green flashes shone from his pie hole, like flickers of a light-up stick or a lightning bug.

"No fucking way," he said.

"Didn't you ever go to sleepaway camp?" I joked.

"No," he said.

I walked over and opened the door, which automatically turned on the light.

He walked over and closed it again and hugged me in the darkness.

"Haze, you make ordinary things seem miraculous to me," he said. "I've never known anyone like you."

I kissed him and we wound up making love on the carpet of the closet floor, among piles of vintage T-shirts, rows of motorcycle boots, and drawers full of sunglasses. If the gar-

ments that hung about our writhing bodies could talk, they
would probably read porn scripts, they'd seen so much. Each
was surely tossed in the corner of some trashed hotel room by
some French-manicured slut, torn over Finn's chest during
his wilder drugged-out days. But now he seemed normal,
more subdued. Into me. Maybe it was a mark of his advanc-
ing age. Maybe he'd outgrown it all. Maybe I would be the
one to tame his roaming nomad-descended heart.

CHAPTER 30

Fantasy is toxic: the private cruelty and the world war both
have their start in the heated brain.
—Elizabeth Bowen

IT WAS OVER BREAKFAST THAT I KNEW HIS OFFER WASN'T
simply an impetuous heat-of-the-moment consideration.

"So Sly is getting you the itinerary this afternoon, but
we're supposed to leave from New York anyway. I have
meetings there and then we fly from Teterboro."

"Okay so . . . you still want me to come?"

"Are you kidding?" he asked, surprised. "Of course! Did
you think I was joking?"

"No, no, I just . . . wanted to make sure you were sure."

"I'm sure. Are you?"

"Yeah!" I leaned over and kissed him and felt such a de-
lightful rush. "My flight home is supposed to be at 4:00 P.M.—"

"Fuck that ticket, you're coming with us!" he said. "We
can leave anytime."

I'd forgotten about his private jet. Ahhhhhhhh, heaven.
I'd flown with Noah on his NetJets charter, and it was pure

heaven versus the stressful airport lines and chaos of LAX and JFK tourist Hades.

We packed our things and while Finn was in the shower, I dialed Noah's cell in Mexico where he'd jetted off post-rager.

"Hey there, my little rock star!" he answered seeing my caller ID.

"Hi, Noah. How's Cabo?"

"Killer. Having a blast. Everyone's still raving about the rager you put on. Good girl, Haze."

"Yeah um, so—"

"What's up?"

"Well . . . I'm feeling a little burnt-out and was wondering if maybe I could take some time . . ."

"Yeah, sure, like a week vacation? You deserve it, babe."

"I was thinking more of like a month or two. A sabbatical. I'm going through some stuff . . ."

"Wow. You okay?"

"Yes, I just need a little time."

"Let's say a month. Paid. You've kicked ass for me, and let's check back in then. Work for ya?"

"YES! That works VERY well. Thank you so much, Noah."

"Hey, Hazel—"

"Yeah?"

"You have fun."

I paused for a minute, remembering him looking over as Finn held my hand in a stolen moment. "Thanks."

He hung up.

I called Kira and filled her in on the plan.

"I'm going to your apartment with Iris after pickup and packing your suitcase. And forget Pop's crusty duffel you have, you're taking my T. Anthony," Kira said.

"Ki, that has your monogram on it."

"Okay, take my Vuitton. You are not going to Europe with The Void with L.L. Fucking Bean."

It was happening. Really happening!

Finn and I got dressed, ran some last-minute errands with Sly, and then picked up his manager, Steve Sharp, who was a smiling Nordic-type guy with a wife and three kids that he left while on the road.

"Hey, you must be Hazel," he said with a handshake.

"Yes, hi! Nice to meet you—"

"We're giving Sean Penn a lift to New York—pop by his place," he instructed Sly, who made a right turn.

I tried to play it cool but EEEEEEEEE! Sean Penn on my plane! I remembered I'd read an interview with him and he had said, "If you want to make God laugh, tell him your plans." And here I was, doing something totally off book, plans out the window, going with the moment.

We pulled into a beautiful driveway and Finn hopped out with Sly and I saw him give the actor a big hug as Sly headed back to the car with his bag. Steve popped out and was on his cell, and I decided to get out and say hello.

I opened the car door and heard Steve's conversation.

"Yeah, we're here by Sean Penn and we got Finn's Flavor of the Month with us and Sly . . ."

Stabs.

I felt punched in the stomach. Hazel, you idiot. Of course there was always some tour bunny accompanying them! Fuck. I spent the rest of the trip silent, and a couple times as the jet fired up, Finn asked me if I was okay.

"Just tired," I said with a half smile.

I napped a little while the guys talked in the front and though the plane was incredibly luxurious, the flight bummed me out more than the rocky roller coaster of our original meeting.

We got to New York and unloaded for the night. There were two cars with drivers waiting, one for just Finn and me, which was a relief, since I found I couldn't even make eye contact with Steve.

When we got in the car, Finn turned to me.

"You were unusually quiet, miss."

Without missing a beat, I told him what Steve had said.

"Oh, Hazel, you're so not that. You're my favorite flavor," he joked. I smiled but still felt unsettled.

"Babe, look. I have a past. Everyone does. But especially in my line of work. I was off the wagon for decades, but I'm on now and I want to ride it with you beside me. Yes, there have been groupies and random hangers-on but I've never invited anyone to travel with me like this. I've had many women but I've never met anyone like you and I know that I never will, sweet girl."

"Really? 'Cause I felt kind of like a faceless skank," I said.

"You are so not! You're brilliant and you know it's not like that—"

"I know. On my side at least. I just want to make sure you really want me to come tomorrow—"

"A hundred percent," he said. "I need my little good witch to come along."

I exhaled, happy. It wasn't really like me to voice my insecurities, but I figured I might as well know before our departure.

"Please stay with me the night? We have the whole top floor of The Standard," he said.

"It sounds amazing," I said. "The view there is great, but I want to kind of hole up with my sister before we go," I said.

"Okay, angel," he said, leaning in for a kiss. "We'll drop you there."

We pulled up to my sister's building and I felt a wave of relief wash over me, as I missed her so much as I always did. She was my vault. Full of whispered sister secrets and confidences kept.

"May I come up and meet her?" Finn asked.

My entire face must have brightened because he added, "I guess that's a yes." I wanted to retrieve my phone to text Kira in case she opened the door with a Pebbles ponytail and terry cloth robe, but sure enough she was her usual knock-out self in a Tory Burch shirtdress and high heels, her blond hair flowing past her shoulders. She was also a much better actress than I was, not revealing the least amount of shock upon seeing her rock star idol standing on her threshold.

"Finn! Hi! Welcome, come on in!"

She was so suave.

"Hi, Kira, nice to meet you—"

"You taking good care of my little sister?" she asked coyly, her brow arched.

"Great care, Kira," I attested, rolling my eyes.

"I hope so. I promise I will," he said with an earnest tone.

"You two are off on quite a voyage," she said, reaching for a bottle of Dom Pérignon. "I think this calls for some champagne."

She popped the cork and filled three flutes as Iris came bounding out in her pajamas and bunny slippers.

"I want some!" she begged.

"Sorry, honey, this is grown-up juice," Kira said as I knelt down and hugged my niece.

"Finn, this is Iris."

"I've heard a lot about you," he said.

"And I've heard ALL about YOU!"

Ahem, thanks, Kira, I said with my eyes as I shot my sister a mock-withering look.

"To The Void," Kira said, looking at Finn, her head tilted to one side. "And hopefully filling it."

I inhaled, semimortified by the presumptuous notion that I was filling any void in the life of Finn Schiller, rock idol.

But before I could hope for a hole in the ground to swallow me up Dr. Evil style, Finn took my hand.

"To filling it."

He lifted his glass and smiled at me midsip, and I felt so excited I thought I'd pass out.

"You sure you two don't want to join us for dinner downtown?" he asked.

I know Kira would've flown the coop in a shot and left the girls with Jack the fucking Ripper as a "caregiver" (as they called it these days), but I interjected before she could start dialing The Babysitters Guild.

"We're sure—" I said, met with a pronounced frown. "I just want to relax a little before we head off tomorrow."

"Okay, angel," Finn said, putting his arm around my waist. He put his glass down and kissed me just as Drew was walking in from work.

"Uh, hey—" he said, confused.

"Hi, oh, hi! Uh, Drew, this is Finn. Finn, this is my brother-in-law, Drew."

"Hey man," he said, shaking Drew's hand as he dropped his briefcase.

"Hi." Drew looked me, then Kira, then Iris, who was grinning ear to ear.

"I should head out," Finn said, opening his arms to hug my sister. "Kira, thank you so much for the drink. I promise to bring her back to you safe and sound," he attested.

"Thank you, Finn," she said, smiling at me over his leather-covered shoulder.

I kissed him good-bye and he got in the elevator.

No sooner did the door close than my phone had a text.

I held it up for Kira as she read aloud.

"I MISS YOU ALREADY."

"OH MY GOD!!!!" she squealed, jumping up and down like a twelve-year-old.

"What is going on?" Drew asked. "Did that just happen?"

"She swore me to secrecy," Kira said. "I'm sorry, honey. But CAN YOU BELIEVE THIS?!"

"What about Wylie?" Iris asked, eyes wide.

We all stood silently for a beat.

"Good question, Iris," Drew said. "What about Wylie?"

"We . . . split up. I wasn't sure and that says something."

"And you're sure about Finn Schiller?" he asked.

"I'm not sure about anything right now." I shrugged. "I have no clue what I want and I'm going to do what Will Applegate wrote on Lexi Brownell's mix tape in high school accompanied with drawings of dancing bears: Surrender to the Flow. It's all I can do."

"Okay. I just hope that 'flow' doesn't hit white-water rapids," Drew said, taking off his coat.

"Drew, I know you love Wylie—" I said.

"I know *you* love Wylie," he said, getting himself a glass of scotch.

Gulp.

I looked at Kira, who reached for the top drawer of Drew's desk, which was overflowing with delivery menus.

"What are we ordering?" she asked.

"Up to you," I said, plopping down on the sofa. I hoped Wylie was okay. I hoped he didn't hate me. I hoped his new restaurant gig would be a big success for him. I was sure it would be, with his talent. And good chefs always get lucky. Always. He would be gobbled up in no time.

The night was spent in front of the TV in the guest room with Kira by my side like the old days when we were roommates. She was on husband safari dating Wall Streeters and working at Sotheby's until she met Drew at a benefit at the Racquet Club, and I was out seeing bands 'til 4:00 A.M. We had intersected rarely in the apartment due to separate social schedules, but on occasion I'd be too hungover to face another night out, and she was getting beauty rest while Drew was away on business, and we'd order in and get in bed and watch John Hughes movies all night. I missed those times, and it was the perfect send-off.

The teenagers in those movies seemed so young to us both—so full of promise, the whole world in front of them. But here I was . . . the same. Nervous, a little insecure, but with the world spread out in front of me. They had no clue what Monday would bring. I had no clue what Monday morning would bring, either. But I was somehow changed in a short time and I knew it.

"My favorite scene—" I said, watching Judd Nelson kiss Molly Ringwald good-bye. She took out her diamond stud and gave it to him. "And now that's me, in a way, with Finn. Even better than Judd. I mean, could you die?"

"I can't even get over it," Kira said, rolling over to face me. She leaned on her hand and looked at me. "You are going to have the best time." I took a deep breath and smiled. "You're living a dream."

"I know," I said. "It's kind of scary. I keep being afraid I'll wake up."

CHAPTER 31

Fantasy love is much better than reality love.
Never doing it is very exciting.
The most exciting attractions are between
two opposites that never meet.
—Andy Warhol

I'M ON A PLANE WITH FINN SCHILLER. AND THIS TIME IT'S
not via upgrade or happenstance or intersecting itineraries.
It's by design; one reservation, two seats first class, side by
side. We are flanked by managers, tour impresarios, peeps.
The whole posse, clad in various rock-star-posse outfits that
looked summoned from central castings wardrobe department, were lifting bags into the overhead, motorcycle jackets open over vintage T-shirts, revealing tattoos and Jolly
Roger belt buckles. Silver wallet chains hung over black
jeans as two of the guys in the band settled into their seats
as one signaled to the other as a hottie blond cheerleader
type walked by in a USC sweatshirt, scanning Finn and
then the girl next to him. Me. Unbelievable.

"You okay?" he asked as I took it all in.

"Yes," I said, exhaling the surreal aspect of this moment. "I just can't believe this. I am kind of in shock. Being back on an aircraft with you. Not by coincidence. It's weird."

"It's great," he said, taking my hand in his and giving it a squeeze. He raised it to his lips and kissed my fingers as a fuzzy rush surged through my entire body. He was so big and cozy and delicious, and while my stomach had unleashed a full-on Lepidoptera convention in my belly, I'd never felt more alive. No guts, no glory, I thought. Here I was, taking a massive leap. I was basically a roadie. Kate Hudson groupie style, minus the smack.

As the passengers streamed into the plane, girl after girl drooled as guy after guy looked away, as if too cool to acknowledge the artist who resided on many of their iPods. I took a deep breath as the door closed and yawnsville announcements began with the cheesy steps to save your life should shit go down. I thought of the JetBlue dude who went shithouse and popped the life raft slides and popped a beer while shooting down. Somehow stories I blow off about various air travel snafus all come flooding to the forefront of my brain when I'm actually in Airbus mode.

"Hazel, this is going to be unforgettable."

"I know. I'm just—"

"Everything is going to be okay. You're going to love it."

The stewardess—oh fuck, sorry—flight attendant, came around with a tray of champagne or orange juice. I took one of each and poured them back and forth, creating a makeshift plastic-cupped mimosa, double fist, no less. "You're afuckingdorable." Finn smiled beholding my ghetto concoction.

"You are," I countered, handing him one. We clinked cheapo barware and took sips with locked eyes. It was the best drink I'd ever sampled.

"How is it?" he asked.

I smiled, swallowing another citrusy bubbly gulp.

"Tastes like adventure."

He put down his drink, and I could hear the familiar sound of his leather jacket scrunching as he leaned into me, a personal machine of worn-in motorcycle garb and zippers and pure man. He softly reached for my face and held my cheek in his hand. I looked at his blue eyes and swore I could feel a tachycardia. Someone pull out the defibrillators. We kissed over the armrest and while midkiss I thought of countless tabloid headlines stalking celebrity tonsil hockey. ("Get a Room, You Two!") I was touched that he didn't even give a shit even as sports jersey–clad buffoons did double takes as they turned sideways to shove down the aisle 'cause they were too obe to do so facing forward. Passenger after passenger including MANY cute girls way younger and cuter than me all stopped to look at Finn . . . then me.

For liftoff we held hands and smiled at each other when the plane had a perfectly smooth glide into the clouds and the pilot assured the cabin we would appear to have smooth skies all the way to Spain.

"Oh good," he said jokingly. "I was afraid you were a bad-luck charm."

"Thanks a lot," I huffed. "I've never had a flight like that before. You brought the tempest with all your fame. You'd have made it a headline and I would have been a sad footnote, like oh, she died on that Void crash."

"Come on, angel, you know you're pure good luck to me," Finn whispered, kissing my cheek.

"Right now I feel like the luckiest girl on the fucking planet. I'm in a Mena Suvari–style bath with four-leaf clovers instead of rose petals."

"You know, Hazel," Finn said, tracing each of my long

fingers with his pointer. "The middle four letters of *clover* are *love*."

"Yes they are!" I marveled. I rarely picked up on the shit that was right in front of my fucking face. I looked at his angular perfect face and suddenly felt like I had a Hannibal Lecter mask to prevent me from blurting it out. I LOVE YOU, FINN! I FUCKING LOVE YOU AND I THINK YOU'RE A FUCKING GENIUS AND I WANT TO FUCK YOU FOR-EVER AND HAVE YOUR BABIES AND DIE IN YOUR ARMS!

But I didn't. Hey, I have some self-control!

"What are you thinking about, sweet girl?" he asked, obviously seeing the Apple computer rainbow wheels a-turnin' in my pupils.

"Huh? Oh, nothing."

Oh, Hazel, you shitty liar.

"Oh really," he pried. "I could've sworn I spied a flicker in there."

I looked out at the cirrus streaks of tire-track clouds out-side the window.

I wanted to throw caution to the wind but I also didn't want to sound like a complete psycho. What was I gonna say? *Oh, hi, platinum recording artist, I know this sounds totally cheeseball and SO tacky Pamela Andersony slash Carmen Electra and Dennis Rodman, but . . . Finn, I love you?* No way!

"I just . . . I'm crazy about you—"

Finn put his finger on my mouth to shush me. "Hazel babe, I'm mad about you, sweet girl."

And with that, I lost my Mile High Virginity.

Okay, I won't glaze over the gory deets, *Twilight*-style. Basically, we kissed so deeply and so intensely that I pulled back, a spark lighting my eye like a tiny cartoon lightbulb connoting a naughty idea. There was a little devil on my shoulder. And over my other shoulder, another devil.

"Finn, I've never done it on a plane."

A huge grin covered his entire face.

"I mean, I'm sure you have, being a rock star and tour constantly and all that shit with countless whores going down on you in lavatories like those red-dotted lines that demonstrate travel across longitudes and latitudes covering all the Rand McNally maps, but—"

"Hazel, I have never done it on a plane."

Huh?

"What? Are you serious?" I guffawed. I didn't know what to say. "I'm sorry, but what kind of fucking rock star are you, anyway?"

He laughed and kissed my hand. "Angel, I am often exhausted, usually with these assholes behind us, and occasionally subject to some journalists' stupid line of questioning."

Without a word, I stood up and walked to the bathroom. No one said a word as Finn casually looked both ways and followed me. Not that anyone noticed or cared, but I stood by the door and said loud enough for no one in particular to overhear, "I don't feel so great. I think I might barf. Finn, can you help me?" I even emitted a little-girl whiney sound I'd never uttered but personally found it Oscar-worthy.

He followed me in, and after we locked the door, which triggered the less-than-flattering fluorescent lights, my two mimosas kicked in and I found myself sitting on the tilted seat cover. I unbuttoned the fly of Finn's jet-black jeans and found him hard and breathless as I took him in my mouth. He was over me, his hands against the plastic panel above me. He groaned and said my name over and over as I felt him harder in my mouth.

"Hazel, I need you," he said, stopping me. He picked me up and bent me over the (tiny) sink and took me. I screamed then giggled as he moved inside me. I tried not to look in the mirror for fear of pores bigger than the cockpit, but I folded my arms over the Lilliputian faucet, so hot for Finn I thought I would explode. He was so amazing, so sexy, so perfect a fit for my body, I almost came when he put his arm around my waist and whispered "Hazel" in my ear as he moved.

As he had me on that sink, at thirty thousand feet, somewhere above the Atlantic, high above the waves and sea creatures and *Titanic*-bow-piercing icebergs and miscellaneous vessels transporting plastic toys or Whac-A-Mole amusement park games or containers of art, I saw stars. To paraphrase Steve Wright, I came like a wildcat.

"Oh my god, oh my god . . . FINN!" I shuddered. I heard him breathless as he turned me around and kissed me almost violently. Our faces were melded as I felt him reach for a paper towel, which he deftly put between my legs to stop drippage.

"I don't want love juice on those hot panties for the rest of the flight," he said. Sexy and practical. How nice. I suddenly got a sad pang, thinking about how Wylie would leap for the tissue box on the bedside table and serve as speediest cum-rag butler on earth. But it passed quickly as I basked in the afterglow of postcoital sky-high euphoria. Me. Finn Schiller. Heaven. Not heaven on earth. Heaven in heaven.

CHAPTER 32

There are some people who live in a dream world,
and there are some who can face reality.
And then there are those who can turn one into the other.
—James Arthur Baldwin

I COULDN'T BELIEVE I WAS IN EUROPE WITH FINN SCHILLER.
We had passports stamped together. We were traveling together, a unit, a duo. His tour managers Jim and Rob were
with us, too, of course, but still. I was in the posse. It was the
ultimate I'm with the band. But not in a slutass follower way.
In a he-loves-me way.

We landed in the Madrid airport and Finn's arm was
around me as the wheels skidded on the tarmac. We deplaned and walked through the surreal new surroundings.
I felt like a poseur with my sunglasses, walking beside the
real rock star, but it was bright and I was puffy. So the Way-
farers came out and along with his peeps, we were greeted
by some weird special fleet of handlers who took my rolling bag from me and insisted on carrying even my shoulder
satchel.

I knew the world was a bunch of fame fuckers but I had no idea it was at this level. I thought there were certain things in life that leveled the playing field—poo, fatigue, customs—but no—everything was expedited. We waited in line for 0.00 seconds as the special airport forces beamed us through. You wanna smuggle a brick of crack? Travel with a celeb. Smuggle that stolen diamond up your ass? Be Finn Schiller's girl. I swear, I could've been wheeling six severed heads in my designer suitcase and I'd've gotten off scot-free.

When we got to baggage claim, we were whisked away in a fleet of SUVs while his "people" stuck around to await the conveyor belt action. I popped a piece of Trident and kissed Finn between wide-eyed visual gulps of the foreign vista spread around me. The greens were different, the signage, the gas stains. Everything was new. And amazing. I could tell when the Queens of Madrid morphed into the Manhattan of Madrid, and soon enough we pulled up to the Ritz Hotel. We didn't even have to check in—a local tour manager met us the moment we revolved through the gilded door, and we were immediately escorted to our massive suite.

"Your crew has the whole floor," we were told as I walked into the room overlooking the entire city. I was in awe.

"Thank god, 'cause that crying baby in the lobby would not have made for a fun neighbor," Finn scoffed.

I drank in the Old World skyline, high on the surreal, pinch-me emotional kaleidoscope I seemed to be looking at life through.

But in the postcardlike vista I started seeing tracers. A tsunami of extreme tiredness engulfed me, and Finn seemed to have read my mind as he pulled me down to him. We kissed and flopped into the majestic four-poster bed. Finn stood up, barely noticing the explosion of flowers, the note from the manager, or the chilled bottle of champagne. He unzipped his jacket and tossed it on a chair next to a huge fruit basket, diving onto the bed. He climbed on top of me, as if he were about to do a push-up over me, and then kissed me before sitting up and looking at his watch.

"I have an interview in a half hour. *Rolling Stone*. I've actually met this journalist before and he's pretty cool, unlike the raging asshole I had grill me last week. These fucking douche bags take everything out of context. Dickholes. They have their agendas, always. But anyway, babe, you nap, sleep tight, I'll be in the living room."

"Are you sure? I feel bad, like, snoozing while you have to work." He seemed stressed-out. Angry. Not at me, just . . . the world. Or something.

"Why? No, fuck no, you rest up, little witch. It's España and we have the show and then a table at midnight. It's okay, I'll nap before we head out for sound check."

Normally when Wylie wanted me to stay up and meet him for one of his chefs' dinners at Blue Ribbon I would moan and groan with forecasted fatigue at the thought of breaking bread in what would technically be the next calendar day, but this time somehow it seemed edgy and exhilarating. As Finn opened his Mac Air and went into the next room, I slid off my jeans and crawled under the covers into luxurious sheets with my T-shirt, pulling my bra out of the sleeve *Flashdance* style.

Holy. Fucking. Shit. I was in Finn's bed. At the Ritz. In Spain. While he spoke to *Rolling Stone* in the next room.

CHAPTER 33

Too much sanity may be madness.
But maddest of all, to see life as it is
and not as it should be.
—Miguel de Cervantes

I DOZED OFF FOR PROBABLY A SOLID HOUR AND AWOKE IN that surreal state of Where the Hell Am I, body tenses, brain confused, only to blissfully recall and slowly melt back into the pillow-topped mattress. Hot fuzzies crept up my groggy spine as I surveyed the surroundings, which looked even more breathtaking than before. Paradise.

I got out of bed and went to the bathroom, brushed my teeth, and walked back out and stood by the enormous wall of windows, quietly absorbing the rooftops. Across the massive bedroom I heard the muted discussion of Finn with *Rolling Stone* through the door. I tiptoed across the carpet and stood by the carved mahogany portal, which was ever-so-slightly ajar. Finn sat on a couch, speaking to the reporter, who sat on an adjacent chaise. I saw the tiny red light of his running recorder, sucking in Finn's words to his devoted masses like a dark gospel of process and song.

"The way I build an album is still rooted in my kind of old-school method where I'm creating the cassette with an A side and B side, a story, really. It's a journey that weaves together as one whole record rather than a ninety-nine-cent single. Even though it won't be consumed like that by most of the fans, there are still some who do kind of absorb it the way I intended, which is cool."

"Interesting. So do you ever hear a single, or the label—"

"Sure, the label always has its ear out for the single, you know, the marketing, whatever. I hear that, I get that it's a machine, I'm not some artist off in fairyland. But I really try to work through the process and yield maybe two albums' worth of songs and then cut and tweak and fix and burn and rebuild so that the net is a solid group of tracks that are thematically interrelated, lyrically, musically, a whole. Like jigsaw pieces."

I had chills. He was so much more interesting and eloquent that any cheesy artist I'd read interviews about. So much more raw and honest. I leaned against the wall to catch a glimpse of him reclining through the sliver the tiny opening offered me.

"To me, an album is only as strong as its weakest track. And I didn't want any of those on *Beggars' Feast*. With this record, I was kind of wresting with the erosion of what I was starting to feel was my youth, you know, being behind me, leaving my thirties, and um, I sensed this time in my life was actually fertile ground for some digging, beyond the pages of my journal—"

"You keep a journal?" the dude asked.

"Oh, yeah, yeah, for years and years. Most of my lyrics, the writing you know, come from in there, I adapt it into rhyming couplets or some other scheme, but um, yeah I write snippets, pieces, kind of seeds of what will inspire me. I tape in images, old postcards. Tons of Polaroids, I hoard all the film I could get my mitts on. I scribble in little notes in the margins. Lately, it's been . . . pretty amazing. We've been recording in a German monastery and it's been one of the most prolific times in my career, actually."

"Really. To what do you attribute that creative spark?"

"Oh god, lots of things. The break from touring, for one. I hung out in California, after touring incessantly and I guess laying low, searching for my next laser-sharp moment kind of fell upon me. I'm kind of in this reckoning phase, growing up, I guess. Also, I uh, I met a girl who blew my socks off."

OH MY GOD. I stepped back from the crack in the doorway. Did he mean ME?! Holyshitholyshitholyshit. I thought I would pass the hell out. Right there on the floor. Someone needed to produce defibrillators. *Moi?* DYYYYYING!

"Oh yeah?" the journalist probed. "Who is she?"

"She's great, we met recently and you know, my life is really kind of a revolving door and people spin in and they spin out and some leave marks on me, some don't. But this one is a fun spin."

Oh.

A *spin*?! That's it? I dropped my life in New York like a flaming paper bag of doody for a SPIN? I darted back to the bed and crawled in. I was in fetal position under the downy comforter, which still didn't comfort me as my head spun like a rainbow Mac wheel. *Maybe it was for show for the guy? To seem mysterious? To sound cool?* It didn't sound cool to me.

I closed my eyes and pretended to be asleep when Finn came back about fifteen minutes later. He quietly undressed and slid under the covers on the other side of the huge bed, and soon enough my feigned slumber became real as I dozed off next to him.

The shrill foreign phone chirp pierced my reverie.

Finn rolled over and groggily answered, looking at his watch. "Fuck, man. Yeah, we're coming. Shit we're going to need sleeping pills tonight, we slept too long . . . yeah man. Thanks."

He rolled over to find my wide eyes staring at him.

"Hi little witch Hazel—" he said.

"Hi."

"What's wrong?"

"Nothing," I responded robotically. "Just tired."

"Let's take a shower together and wake the hell up," he said, leaning on me. I felt so vulnerable there, wondering how many other girls had come along for the ride. Showered with him. Flipped on their backs when he snapped. Catered to his moods when someone was a "dickhole." How many others jumped excitedly on his beds, pinched themselves beneath the covers, and fell giddily asleep beside him. Fuck it: I was not a weak link in his chain of fools.

And then I figured: fuck it, I was thirty. Why play games? It was all or nothing at this point in myself and I refused to coyly step through the minefield of his deified stature and the statistics of all who came before me.

"Finn, I didn't mean to eavesdrop," I began with mild trepidation. I took a deep breath and my resolve crystallized. "But I was coming out of the bathroom and . . . I heard what you said about my being a little 'spin' in your Macy's door. It didn't make me feel that great, to be honest. I know I sound foolish and have zero claim to your affections beyond . . . the spin, or whatever this is, but somehow it made me feel really stupid and insignificant."

"Oh god, sweetheart, no." Alarmed. "You're not that. At all," he said, touching my cheek. "I need to say that because if I go on about you, they'll stalk you, drive us nuts. I need to play it down. But if that makes you feel weird or insignificant—which you are not—I can kiss you at Bernabéu Stadium tonight in front of everyone. And I will. I'll pull you onstage and kiss you for all of them. I was trying to protect you. I've never met anyone like you."

I exhaled, fears instantly assuaged. "No, it's okay. I get it, I guess. I don't need to be your girlfriend. I just didn't want to be . . . another Polaroid in your book."

"I don't know quite what you are. You're so much more than a Polaroid. So much more than the others who have toured with me. All of them. I'm just . . ."

"What?" I asked, noticing his brow, which furrowed in stress like the fateful wind-tossed day we met.

"I'm not a good . . . boyfriend. Lover. Whatever you want to label it. I always fuck it up. I get ants in my pants. I need to move and evolve."

"I don't need to label it." I nodded, feeling semidumb at instigating the whole "what are we doing here" typical girl convo. "I just didn't want to be some faceless whore groupie, because I'm not."

"Of course you're not." He laughed. "Those never last more than a few hours let alone weeks on end," he said.

Great. So he did have faceless groupie whores. *Wait . . . Hazel, of course he did, he's a fucking rock star! One who used to do drugs nonstop as he confessed to you, you moron! Calm down.* I cleared my envious throat. "I just want to enjoy this, whatever it is, each day, wherever it leads."

"We will," he said, pulling my hand to his lips. He kissed my fingers and then pulled me toward him, and our warm mouths met for the sweetest of kisses.

"You ready to come rock the Old World?"

"Ready," I said, sitting up to get dressed.

"We have sound check and then I'm going to ravish you in my dressing room," he said tauntingly.

"Promise?"

"Swear to god."

CHAPTER 34

In my fantasy I was always the savior.
I would come to Peanuts *land and save everybody.*
Charlie Brown would fall madly in love with me.
Peppermint Patty was so jealous.
—Alicia Witt

BERNABÉU STADIUM WAS ON ITS FEET. I STOOD FROM THE wings and danced with Rob, who twirled me around, and I can honestly admit, I'd never had a high quite like that. The throngs had lungs half-shrieked out.

"AND THIS IS NOTHING NEXT TO WEMBLEY!" Jim screamed over the deafening hordes.

I couldn't believe it. What a majestic scene. Everyone there was frenzied, high, moving as if electrocuted. Eyes were closed, mouths open with song or yells. Women wore bras, men thrashed, couples played tonsil hockey.

Though I was removed up on the royal perch of stage left, the sweat and heat and throb of the pulsating bodies engulfed me. Their fever was an all-encompassing contagion. I was in awe as I scoped the masses.

Rob took my hand and poured me a shot.

"Cheers, Hazel. You're not like the others," he said.

"Awesome! Not an anonymous trollop? Terrific!"

We clinked shot glasses and I swigged the liquid and felt it instantly.

Finn's pummeling guitar ravaged my heart and I felt my blood pressure rise (and my panties moisten!) when he winked at me from the mic. All those girls—some ten, twelve years younger than me, and he kept turning to the side and looking at me.

After awhile he stopped to introduce the band, and after each name came a smattering of applause. Then he looked at me and pointed. My cheeks grew flush and I instantly looked behind me to see if Rob or someone was there. I was like Molly Ringwald exiting the church with Jake Ryan standing there, leaning against his Porsche. *ME?* No . . . I nodded, as if to say no way.

"She's being shy," Finn said sweetly with a puppy dog face, "but this one is for my girl."

The yellow guitar pick hit the strings and I knew from the first chord it was "Frost." A surge jolted through me as my hand found itself upon my spastic ticker; if Kira could only be here now . . . we used to lie awake at night playing his power ballad, telling each other romantic stories until we fell asleep.

It encrusted my core
Strangled my soul
Cut off the air
My body was coal
The frost
The frost
It slowed my pulse

It made me gasp
It killed my joy
I was in death's grasp
And then came you
You melted the frost
You kissed away the gloom
A quicksand of doom
I'd thought all was lost
You chiseled away
The frost
The frost . . .

I swayed to the sexual grinding of the bass and couldn't believe my ears. Or eyes. Even the smell—big-time pot in the air and the stench of spilled beers and body odor—normally none too appetizing—felt amazing. My arm hairs stood on end. The aged scotch hung on my brain, and my brain saw a kaleidoscope of swirling lights in every hue. When a color changed, the memory of the last bulb stayed with me, until the point where each blink brought a majestic palette of former shined wattage. It was youth and music and all my senses were appealed to. I made a mental note to Xerox this moment with my whole being. A memory CT scan. Life didn't get more alive than this.

CHAPTER 35

Heaven knows, I've exposed myself in my novels
through the use of fantasy and imagination . . .
now my new book is about what
really happened to me . . . not my heroines.
—Judith Krantz

PARIS FOLLOWED. ON THE PLANE, WHILE FINN WAS IN A
meeting, I checked my e-mail and filled in the gang, who
all had sent worried e-mails wondering WTF. No one could
believe our little parlor game had managed to be home-
wrecking. And then after perusing the latest J.Crew eblast,
a new e-mail popped up. That was odd—it was the dead of
night in New York. I opened it up and my heart stopped.
Wylie.

> Dear Hazel, Don't worry: not here to stalk or
> boil rabbits or anything. I just wanted to lob
> a little platonic pebble to your cyber window in
> the hopes that down the road we can at the very
> least be friends, catch up with a late night

soufflé, or even just e-mail from time to time.
I miss you in my life, and even if it means
seeing you once in awhile (or having to endure
your wearing some Finn Schiller tour T-shirt) it
would just make me happy to be in touch. Even if
we aren't Velcros, you will always be my lucky
charm. xoWy.

To try and stave off any tears I blamed the rising lump in
my throat on travel fatigue and I closed my laptop and then
closed my eyes.

I awoke in the City of Lights, another nation of fame
fuckers who ushered us through customs with ease into
an awaiting Maybach. A suite at the Ritz was opened with
majestic double-height double doors. There were peonies
from Lachaume sent by Karl Lagerfeld, a friend of Finn's,
chilled champs waiting, and a personal note from the manager ribboned onto a basket of fruit that could feed a Ugan-
dan village. For brunch, we ordered rich hot chocolates
and butter-soaked scrambled eggs that were a yellow fluffy
bullet to the *coeur* but worth every ambrosial bite.

"Tonight we have dinner with Johnny and Vanessa,"
Finn said casually.

"Um . . . like . . . Depp and Paradis?"

"Oui, mon ange."

He laughed at my starstruck self and leaned over the
bed to kiss my forehead.

I got a quick pang of sadness thinking of Wylie's and
my Double Dog Dare game where we'd go up to a celeb
and compliment them on their amazing performance in one
of their bombs. You wouldn't do it to, say, Meryl Streep in
She-Devil (though let the record reflect that I fucking LOVE
that movie, forced on me by Kira at 2:00 A.M., no less) but

more like obnoxious peeps. I happened to WORSHIP Johnny Depp, even though it's kind of weird for a grown man to be named Johnny, but he was sealed into the Pantheon forever and ever. But I mean what would Finn do if I hailed his *21 Jump Street* days?

I was giddy all day. We met the famed couple at La Société and it was weird having passersby survey the table and notice that I was the only nobody. They were both perfectly lovely and I'm happy to say I held my own, though I freakishly SMS'd Kira beforehand with enough OMGs to beat out a high school full of texting teens.

"So Finn, where you are recording next?" Vanessa smiled. "Not back to that funeral parlor, *non*?"

"No, no." Finn shook his head. "I'm done with that. I think next we'll hit this abandoned sake brewery in Japan. I heard the acoustics are amazing, and after that monastery I can't go back to a lifeless studio, it's canned and manufactured. I have Charles, ya know, in Tokyo and he always hooks us up and this place is apparently just awe inspiring."

Japan? A sake brewery? I wasn't quite sure if I fit into the "we" in the "we'll go" equation. I found myself being sort of a mute the second half of dinner.

We went back to our magnificent suite at the Ritz facing the Place Vendôme and I looked at the carved obelisk in the center as I let the chilled night air wash over me. Finn was tinkering in the bathroom and soon I felt his arms around my waist and his lips lightly dotting the back of my neck. His feather-light kisses sent chills up my arms to my shoulders as he magnified the goose bumps but delicately slid one of the thin satin straps from my nightgown.

We made love. I'd been insecure about my blowj skills, because for some reason, probably common sense, I'd suspected or rather known for shizzle, that countless groupies had given him killer head. But again, my what-the-heck guts kicked in, and I went for it.

"Bewitched again, Hazel. You are a world-class fellatrix."

"Oh really?" I grinned coyly. (Yes!)

He grabbed me and tackled me to the bed and we fell asleep in a cuddleball.

The next day was press galore for Finn and some shopping for me. I raided the Bonpoint *soldes* outlet for the nieces and scored myself a couple cute blouses, and made my way back to the hotel in the light drizzle. The color gray never looks as beautiful as it does in Paris. Moody yet soft, complementing the rooftops yet a stylish pop all its own. I swung my shopping bags in the spring rain and turned back to the Ritz circle.

How strange to walk these cobblestones in such a different way. I'd been to the famed hotel years back with Wylie. We just wanted to see it and could never afford to stay there, or even dine, so we splurged on a round of drinks in the Hemingway Bar, strolling the long hallway of vitrines and gawking at the chic crowd.

"Who are these people?" Wylie had mused as we looked at our fellow drinkers. "That guy has to be a Greek shipping magnate. And that woman is a Russian oil heiress. And there, that's gotta be a Bond villain of some sort."

We spied Valentino Garavani with his boyfriend and a half dozen models. I had been staring at the beautiful lines of their silhouettes.

"You're way more beautiful," Wylie had said, taking my hand.

I rolled my eyes, as if to say bullshit.

He turned my hand over and traced a heart on my wrist with his finger, then kissed my pulse.

I snapped back to the moment walking into the revolving doors just as the rain picked up and the drops thickened. I'd have just a bit of time to lie down for a half hour then change for the concert.

Once again the crowd was deafening. The whole experience was so surreal and yet somehow still felt intimate, since Finn would often turn to his left and smile at me. During his break before the encore, he took me sweaty in his arms and kissed me, but then was grabbed by handlers and roadies the second he got offstage.

I didn't see him for an hour as he was whisked away to greet Charlotte Gainsbourg and her lover, plus some other French bigwigs—the children of an ambassador, some Légion d'honneur dude, and some big deal actress there. I was on the side, and was warmly greeted by Johnny and Vanessa, which was my only source of comfort, as I felt slightly invisible in the backstage throng of well-wishers, all of whom had credentials and seemed to know Finn quite well, judging by the bear hugs aplenty.

Finally the last of the contest winners, record execs, and local MTV peeps petered out with the main promoter, and we were told the car was outside. We piled in, exhausted. Boy was I ready to pass out.

"The after party is in the marvelous old titty bar in the Bastille!" Rob exclaimed.

After party? Oy to the vey.

"We'll just stop by," Finn whispered, holding my hand in the backseat, sensing my reluctance somehow in my pulse.

The joint was packed with beautiful people, fashionistas, designers, some famous poet, not that I knew poets could be famous these days, but I guess if not in France then where? I sat and talked with Jim for a bit about the Asian leg, which was coming together, and glanced at my watch. 3:00 A.M. Oh, brother.

Finally Finn was fading a bit and we were off to London the next morning, so we headed back to the Ritz.

As I walked inside toward the elevators I saw a twenty-something couple emerge from the Ritz bar in blue jeans, holding hands, giggling. I wondered if they had splurged on a drink. Or were playing a game of what's their story, or were ogling Finn. I watched them leave until they exited, as the guy put his arm around his girl and kissed her temple.

"Hazel?"

I turned when I heard Finn calling me from the open elevator and I quickly followed his voice.

CHAPTER 36

In fantasy, you can make a complete break,
and you can put people in a situation where
they are confronted with things that they
would not confront in the real world.
—Elizabeth Moon

IN THE RAINY THICK MIST OF THE SHADOWY LONDON
streets, Finn Schiller and I held hands. He felt even warmer
in the damp air. We roamed tiny alleyways and stepped
over puddles, with chilled cheeks and a natural cerulean
light that was exactly like the look in his haunting, romantic
videos. The twilight electric blue sky was so atmospheric it
was as if we were underwater but breathing oxygen, blue
and moody, cooling and crisp.

"I mean, don't you feel like we are on the set of *Sweeney
Todd*?" I asked him. "Hopefully we won't be churned into
mincemeat pies."

"Tim Burton's a great friend."

Pause. Throat clearage. "You know him?"

"Yeah, yeah, he digs the music. We'll have dinner with him and Helena when we get to New York."

My fave director. The heart stops.

Then it sank a bit, thinking of facing New York, my home. I had just been pretending it wasn't there for the time being.

Finn put his arm around me and kissed my forehead as we walked down a pathway lined with gaslit lanterns, glowing orange in the quick-ebbing remains of daylight.

"What's that?" I asked, noticing a glowing square of window in a small stone carriage house with intriguing signage. It was a white painted wooden carving of an open book with German black-letter font hand-painted on it: *Ex Libris.*

"Let's check it out," Finn said. As we crossed the damp cobblestones, we passed a couple of London hipsters who did a whiplashing double take when they spotted who he was. He didn't even notice or at least didn't acknowledge their points and whispers as he opened the door to the store, put his hand on the small of my back, and guided me inside. The cozy Hogwartsian set piece I discovered inside was perfection. A hundred-year-old shop, complete with stone mantel and wood-burning fireplace, was out of a dream. And books, books, books, old, new, piled high. There was almost a whiff of magic, though nothing sinister, just charmed. I inhaled the aroma of crackling burned wood and musty pages to the ceiling's ancient mahogany rafters, lined with sliding ladders.

"This place is incredible," I marveled to the bespectacled guy reading behind the counter.

"Thank you ever so much," he said in a crisp British accent as he put down the tattered tome he was reading. "It's been my family's business for over a hundred years."

"I can tell," I said, exploring little nooks and crannies, each divvied into makeshift sections, cooking, fiction, painting, photography, poetry.

"Oh my gosh!" I exclaimed, noticing a section of first edition children's picture books. "You have first editions of all these Shel Silverstein books?!"

"He's the best. Best there ever was," the owner said.

"Who's that?" Finn asked.

"Wait . . . are you serious? You don't know Shel Silverstein?"

"No. I didn't exactly get read to as a kid."

"I love these books. I lived for them as a child."

"Let me get them for you then," Finn said.

"No, no, really. I'm going to buy these two, *The Missing Piece* and *The Giving Tree*, my two favorites. I loved the poems as well, but somehow I kept returning to the narratives and haven't read them in ages."

"We'll take these two," Finn said, taking the copies from my hand and placing them on the counter with his credit card.

"Really?" I said, feeling slightly odd.

"H, it is my pleasure." His eyes flashed and his black hair shone in the firelight.

"Thank you. So much. I really love these and will cherish them always."

We got my wrapped-up package tied with twine (worship!) and walked back outside to find in the minutes we wandered the store it had become night. We headed back to the hotel, where hordes of people roamed the pristine lobby, all craning when they noticed Finn.

"Finn! I need you," Steve, his manager, said, closing his cell and bolting over. "I have the promoters of the Australian leg of the tour in the bar. Can I steal him for a sec?" he asked me.

"Of course, sure," I said, surprised he would even ask me.

"I'll see you upstairs," Finn said over the shoulder of his leather jacket as he was led off by Todd.

I went up to the massive suite, not believing people actually traveled this way. I took off my clothes, put on the deliciously cozy Pratesi robe hanging in the bathroom, and climbed into the downy cloud that was the linen-sheeted bed from heaven.

At the foot of the bed, I noticed my brown-paper-wrapped books. Summoning what energy I had left from our long walk, I leaned forward to retrieve it and leaned back on my bevy of fluffy pillows as I delicately unwrapped the paper. *The Missing Piece* was on top.

I flipped through the pages, loving the simple black ink images that were still familiar to me after twenty-five years. That's when you know you're old, when a memory triggered seems like yesterday when it was, in fact, decades old. The protagonist, a large proto-Pac-Man with one slice of pie missing, is rolling around, searching for the sliver with just the right fit. One is too big, another is too small. Some are misshapen, some don't fit at all. And then he finds the One. The one that fits perfectly. They click, they fit, they roll. They explore the world together.

And then . . . I realized as I kept turning the pages my memory had failed me. It was twenty-five years ago, and not yesterday.

In my weathered recollections of the story, worn by the pumice of years and years, I somehow had thought they rolled off into the sunset. Wrong.

He gently sat the piece down. Then rolled off alone, singing, "I'm looking for my missing piece . . ."

Huh. Kira was right . . . the ending was kind of sad. Bizarre! I mean, why did I love that so much? I suppose as an innocent child there weren't any romance-tinged metaphors associated with the plain, simple story, so it never would have occurred to me that it was even remotely laced with wistful melancholy. But he moves on. Looking for that next piece. Searching in the first page, searching in the last page.

Hmm. I closed the book and pulled out the one that was lying beneath it. *The Giving Tree.* Another simple black-pen-on-white-paper illustrated book about a tree and a little boy. The tree loved nothing more than giving. When the boy is little it gives him its branches to climb on, its apples to eat. Later in his adulthood, the tree gives him its wood to make a house.

As I got to the end, where the boy is now an old man, needing a place to sit, I welled up a little reading how the tree, now just a stump, offers itself as a seat.

"And the tree was happy."

I closed the book as I leaned back for a nap, and when I shut my eyes, two tears spilled out.

CHAPTER 37

Fantasy is the only canvas large enough for me to paint on.
—Terry Brooks

WHEN I WOKE UP, IT WAS TIME FOR A QUICK SUPPER BEFORE what would be the biggest concert of the tour. Finn dove on the bed and tickled me awake, and I warmed to his embrace as he kissed me into consciousness. I had to get up, but before I headed to the bathroom I lay down on top of him, somehow trying to replicate human blanket.

"Ow!" he said, when I smashed him.

"Oh my god, I'm so sorry, did I crush you?"

He winced. "No, no, it's fine. Just didn't see that coming."

I felt a surge of embarrassment. "I'm so sorry—"

"No, no—" He put a hand on my bashful cheek. "Come here."

He leaned in and kissed me. I felt a strange fear, like I was in such unchartered territory, making my own history on the voyage, experiencing it all alone in my head.

I showered and dressed, heading downstairs to an

awaiting car, which whisked us to Daphne, one of his favorite restaurants. We drank a sumptuous bottle of Bordeaux and chowed, sharing each other's dishes, when his phone rang. It was one of his reps in L.A.

He nodded and asked a couple questions, then hung up.

"What was that?" I asked.

"Ugh, another offer for a movie sound track. Some romantic comedy bullshit."

"That's cool! Have you ever wanted to do a sound track? I bet you would be amazing at it! So many of the songs on *The Spirits* are so cinematic, and they don't have lyrics, so I always kind of picture my own movie scenes . . ."

"Nah, that's all too happy-go-lucky for me. I'd do a horror movie, maybe. But even those have happy endings. Some kind of salvation for the one poor schmuck who makes it out alive."

"What's wrong with a happy ending?" I asked, thinking of my own hatred of movies that end with bodies everywhere and no sunset to ride off into. "Have you ever tried to make music that's infused with some of the joy you clearly derive from life?"

"I do love my life, I do . . . but . . . it's boring to sing about that. Let everyone else revere the bluebirds and love and all that shit."

I paused. "Love is shit?"

"Not all of it . . ." He shrugged, almost blasé, as if we were talking about something completely benign, like sandwiches.

"What about that ballad you did . . . 'Delilah'?" I probed. Kira and I always wondered who this Delilah person was. Clearly he'd been smitten ("My molten heart, you wrenched apart").

"Oh, she wasn't real," he said, shaking his head. "I never name anything for real people. They always leave or change or disappoint."

I nodded quietly. Was he lying?

"It's just . . . you know when a funny actor who makes you laugh decides to go and get a serious role to win an Oscar?" he asked.

"Yeah, I hate that," I confessed.

"Well, that's how my fans would feel if I suddenly got all happy-go-lucky, extolling the virtues of amore. They take comfort in my songs because it's a safe place for them. Their anguish or loneliness or suffering feels understood. You should see the letters I get, the e-mails. These kids, or their parents, or whoever feels like the anguish in their soul mirrors mine and it makes them feel less alone in the universe."

"That's true, and I'm glad—you sure as hell did that for me and legions of others. But you're not put here only to serve as their mirror, you're also your own person who can evolve. Honestly, I think it's all just a safe place for you. You're so used to being in that cave that it hurts to crawl out and see the sunlight. It's easier to play that role."

"Right." He shrugged matter-of-factly. "Like Jim Carrey being the goofball. But I still want him as the goofball and not the tortured soul. It's the opposite for me. I'd rather subvert my own glee and keep the music rooted where it started."

"That's absurd." I laughed, with a tinge of frustration. "That's cutting off your nose to spite your face. Why not try and allow yourself to be free of all the torment? Just try it. It's not so bad out there on the other side."

"No thanks," he said, patting my head. "I like it in the cave better."

He stood up and reached for me to take his hand, which

I did. But as we walked off—Finn preparing to face his legions upon scores of screeching fans, people who wept at his lyrics, his throaty vocals and grinding riffs because he yanked their own heartstrings along with the steel guitar ones, I thought of Wylie. The one who didn't believe in the transience of loved ones. The one who named his restaurant for me. The girl he wanted to make his wife. Who sprinted from a precious proposal and threw herself into a man who wanted only wings and change and constant evolution.

I couldn't live in a cave. I needed the warmth of hope, of family, of the toasty blanket of reveling in giving love and being cherished. Flying with him to London had given me wings. But suddenly . . . I needed roots.

CHAPTER 38

Fantasy mirrors desire. Imagination reshapes it.
—Mason Cooley

THE SET WAS INDEED LEGENDARY. WEMBLEY STADIUM HELD ninety thousand people, most of whom were absolutely devoted from day one, along with teens who discovered The Void later in life. I swayed in the wings, relishing the final chords of "Black Wings," singing along like a loser groupie but one who knew she had her own road that didn't overlap with the tour bus. As the deafening applause roared through the massive area, Finn took off his guitar and ran offstage. Rather than go for the water, he came right for my waist, which he encircled with his sweaty arms, giving me a huge kiss. It was a rush. The would-be apex of life for any fan, any girl. But somehow I felt a tightness in my throat that rivaled the thrill quotient. As beseeching shrieks for an encore blasted my eardrums, Finn toweled off, swigged some Evian, and kissed my forehead quickly. Then he gave me a quick wink and headed back onstage to the microphone as the ocean of exhausted larynxes gave a screaming push of final noise that could have easily registered on the Richter scale.

"This one is for my little H."

The famous opening chords of "Salt Water" sounded to a welcoming rumbling of claps and hollers. His voice dragged liltingly over the opening lyrics.

> *My thoughts are dotted with you,*
> *I am besotted, this gutting true.*
> *It's like I swallowed a wrench,*
> *My fists are always clenched,*
> *If I lose you, I lose me*
> *If I lose you, I lose me*
> *Adrift to drown in this black sea.*
> *Salt water in my wound*
> *Salt water in my wound*
> *Your notes to mine are too attuned*
> *Salt water in my wound*
> *Your absence's like lifting a boulder*
> *This ache's a pain I cannot shoulder*
> *We once could only burn and smolder*
> *But now I'm pelted by freezing rain*
> *You tripped a wire I can't explain*
> *If I lose you, I lose me*
> *Adrift to drown in this black sea.*
> *Salt water in my wound*
> *Salt water in my wound*
> *Your notes to mine are too attuned*
> *Salt water in my wound*
> *If I lose you, I lose me*
> *If I lose you, I lose me*

As his voice trailed and almost seemed to slowly lick each seductive word as it spilled from his lips through the silver grid of the mic's interlaced wires, his hot breaths filled the unseasonably chilly English air. Practically inaudible now, his final words, a whispered *If I lose you, I lose me*, slithered out like a drawn-out, beckoning plea, so quiet yet screaming and blazing with a zillion decibels of emotion. I felt a tear spill out of my left eye and roll down my cheek.

I reached up to wipe it, but as a breeze blew, I felt the wind on the track my own salt water had left on my face; as the wind hit the wet line it was like a highlighter to my emotions. Crying, feeling, understanding. I got it. I knew it was safe to feel anguish, I knew it was a place I could always retreat to, courtesy of Finn.

But I also knew it was braver in a way to get it out—not wipe it away but let it roll off my chin to my chest, burrowing its way inside, where it would always remain along with Finn. But the braver thing to do, stronger than curling up in that cave, is to armor up and face the music, as it were. And that was just what I needed to do. I looked out at the faces and felt the hum of their cheers, but rather than looking out at them, I retreated into myself, as if I were in a library and not a jam-packed stadium. This was amazing—all of it—but would 342 stadium shows start to blend into one? What about coziness with the remote control and a yummy dinner? I thought about my desperate longing to yank apart the Velcros and suddenly missed smashies and human blanket desperately. I looked down at my feet, countless serpentine wires winding all around plugged into amps and stuck down with yellow tape. My black boots didn't feel like they were meant to tiptoe over those electric cables forever. I tiptoed back into the wing and sat down, watching the encore.

After the show, Finn and I went into his dressing room

so he could wash up before a dinner in London. After his shower, he came out refreshed as I sat on a blue couch as hordes of VIPs awaited his majesty on the other side of the door.

"I'm starving. I could use one of those food fuel pills right about now," he teased as he toweled off his ripped torso.

"Finn, I'm . . . not coming to dinner. I mean, I'm not coming along. For the rest of the tour. I need to go see my sister," I stammered. "I need to go home."

Finn stopped getting dressed and looked at me with a witheringly disappointed glance that then fell to the floor. "I know."

I stood up and crossed the room to hug him.

"I knew you wouldn't stay, Hazel. And I understand. You're too delicate for this shitty nomadic life. This whole world, you're too good. Too beautiful," he added stoically.

"Finn, this has been . . . a dream come true." I started to cry. "I can't even get over what this whirlwind has been. Just now . . . onstage, that was akin to a religious experience or something . . ." I shook my head. "But I have my real life, and I miss my sister. I have never gone this long without seeing her."

"I understand," he said, though we both sort of knew that as an only child and an orphan . . . he didn't.

"You and I," I started, choking up. "We are on different pages of different books on different shelves in different languages . . . I just don't know how I could foresee enmeshing myself completely into your world without relinquishing so much of what makes mine tick."

"And I would never want you to," he said, taking my hand in his. He took his other hand and put it upon my cheekbone, sloughing off the armies of tears that had gathered there. "I'll never ever forget you," he promised.

More tears flowed as I looked into his enormous blue eyes. I put my hand on his hand that wiped a new spill of salty water off my cheekbone and took a deep breath. I wasn't facing the music, I was walking away from it.

"Never ever," I said, hugging him good-bye.

The car to Heathrow was strangely not filled with convulsive sobs but rather a few more streams of controlled tears and then . . . oddly . . . relief. Like a sliver of silver moon appearing from behind the werewolfey thick clouds, so did my own self. Not the impetuous rebel Hazel who dashed off, abandoning her personal galaxy like a rogue comet, but one who was homey, who loved watching *30 Rock* and *South Park,* putting her feet up on the couch with Glad Corn and Martinelli's sparkling cider. Who loved food, and didn't ever want it replaced by a pill. Who loved her friends, real friends instead of paid friends. And laughter and dirty jokes and other music that was sometimes cheesy or goofy or even (gasp!)—pop. Music that made me feel just plain old cheerful rather than "understood."

I went through passport control with my bag and coach ticket and found at the gate that HLAVERY was up on the check-in screen. I approached the desk.

"Yes, ma'am, delighted to inform you that your upgrade came through!" chirped the blond Brit in uniform.

"Oh, great," I said, not even really caring, though a wider seat was always a plus.

"There you are, ma'am. Seat 3B."

Of course. What goes around comes around. I couldn't believe it! And yet, somehow, I could.

"Thank you very much."

I sat in the gate waiting area for a few minutes until they preboarded my section. I walked the jetway, found my seat, and put my bag overhead. I plopped down and opened a magazine, looking at the stream of incoming passengers, wondering who would sit beside me. A tall African American woman smiled at me but then saw that she was the row behind, in 4B. Next an anal businessman glanced at the number above my head but moved on. And then, just my luck, a dad with a ten-month-old boy in a BabyBjörn. Greaaaaat. Just what I needed for seven hours!

I smiled a half smile in greeting as he deftly maneuvered his gear into the overhead compartment, then unstrapped the baby and plopped him on his lap for takeoff.

"Apologies in advance," the man offered in his clipped queen's English. "I'm afraid Benji and I are your flying companions this evening, I'm terribly sorry for any fidgeting or crying but I vow to do my best." He grinned warmly. Benji's brown eyes sparkled as his smile met my own.

"He's precious. Really," I said, swearing I could almost see a cartoon twinkle in his spirited retinas. "He looks like he was chiseled off the Sistine Chapel ceiling," I said.

"You're too sweet, thank you," the dad said.

"No it's true, he's like a little angel . . . ," I said as the baby gripped my index finger. Suddenly I felt a wave of emotion crash over me. The dad noticed that I suddenly seemed a bit choked up.

"Are you all right?" he asked.

"Yes, yes, I'm fine," I said, reinforcing my emotional levees with a couple deep breaths. "Just excited to see my family is all."

"They're in New York?" he asked.

"Yes, well my sister, Kira, is picking me up and we're going out to her house in East Hampton."

"How lovely."

I nodded.

The duo began to watch Warner Bros. cartoons full of

Road Runner's beep-beep honking mischief and loads of explosives, and I instantly thought of an e-mail Wylie had sent me on our first anniversary.

Happy anniversary, Hazel. A whole year, and I still feel like my skeleton is forged in iron and you are a huge ACME Products cartoon magnet from Wile E. Coyote's arsenal. I'm never going to stop feeling uncontrollably drawn to you, it's hard-wired into my bones. I'm yours. Wylie.

As my eyelids grew heavy, Benji's dad shut down the portable DVD player, and mirroring his fresco da Vinci self, Benji was an absolute cherub, drifting off to sleep on his daddy's lap. And shortly after, I was also adrift in slumber that lasted until the plane was descending.

I awoke stiff but a bit refreshed, realizing only then that I hadn't slept very well in the last month.

"Look who's up, Benji? Your girlfriend!"

I smiled and took his little fat hand in mine as we prepared for landing. "He was incredible," I said, praising his proud father.

"I know! And I can say that because he's never this easy," he confessed. "You were our lucky charm."

A sting of sharp acid tears pierced my eyes anew as I leaned to look out my window as the lights of New York beckoned below, spread out like a terrestrial blanket of stars as miraculous as the ones that shined above. This city, made by man from nothing, ignited more marvel in me than the map of lights that glistened in the sky. Home.

I was practically on fire, gathering my things as I wished the cute father and son a good visit, and ran off the plane. Benji. That face, that giggle, those eyes, their twinkle. Finn never wanted that, ever. The world was too crushing for him, too evil, too suffocating, and yet the child cooed and smiled and slumbered his way across a restless angry ocean, peaceful and pleased as pie.

I ran off the jetway. That was never Finn's vision for his life, never his desire. He couldn't see in the Sistine Ceiling the colorful bursts of pigment, only the falling plaster and decay of buildings, rather than their majesty. Benji's spasmodic laughter, rivaling the YouTube baby's in sheer cuteness, wasn't Finn's dream.

It was Wylie's.

Ferreting through the crowd of rolling suitcase–lugging drones, I wove in and out of the onslaught of fanny packs, rummaging my way past packed newsstands and socks-and-sandals people and Yankees T-shirt shops. Past a blur of green souvenir Statues of Liberty, I ran, down to passport control, flying through customs.

I had nothing to declare.

I had everything to declare.

I burst through the double doors as hundreds of eyes of excited family members awaited their loved ones back from abroad. In the United Nations melting pot, I heard my name. I turned to see Kira, waving frantically.

"Hazel! Here, honey!!"

I ran to her and hugged her madly.

"Yaaaay! You're home!!!!!" she shrieked.

"Not yet," I said soberly, looking into her blue eyes. "I can't come to the Hamptons," I said.

The corners of her mouth slowly widened as she exhaled a happy sigh.

"Go get 'em."

CHAPTER 39

How much research I have to do depends
on the nature of the story. For fantasy, none at all.
—Alan Dean Foster

IT WAS THE LONGEST TAXI RIDE OF MY LIFE. FINALLY, AT
Ludlow and Houston, I threw a wad of cash at Mohammed
Mohammed, the driver, then opened the door and ran out. I
could see my breath in the night air as my legs ran me as fast
as they could. I've never done heroin, but in that moment
of running to see him again, I felt like a junkie sprinting to
meet her dealer, waiting to cook up the smack in the spoon,
tie the tourniquet on my arm, fill the needle slowly, and surrender my soul to utter bliss once more. I've never craved
anything in my life as much as him. Not schlong per se, but
heart; his arms around me, my head on his chest again, safe.
I was fiending, pacing, agasp. I needed him in the marrow
of my bones. And I prayed I could get my fix once more. I
had the perfect life and it turned course so drastically, as if
overnight. I ached inside. But I guess they call it growing
pains for a reason.

I was standing in his labor of love, his new restaurant,
Hazel, with my heart in my hands.

"You know Shel Silverstein?" I asked, like a raving ranting psycho.

"Of course. Who doesn't?" Wylie asked, wondering what the hell crack pipe I had been sucking on. "Hazel, are you okay?"

I knew I probably looked like a total freak, having deplaned from a transatlantic flight with nary a hairbrushing.

"Some people are always looking for his missing piece. They'll always be looking, searching, brooding. The quest, the tour, the road, is his life. But you, Wylie—" My voice cracked as I looked into his brown eyes. "You are the Giving Tree."

"What are you talking about?" he asked, putting a worried hand on my shoulder. "Hazel . . ."

"Wylie, I am so sorry I freaked out. I should have my head examined. I have behaved like a selfish, juvenile lunatic. And I know you probably detest me, but all I know is that I am madly in love with you. I need you."

I started to cry as I took his hand in mine and knelt down on the floor of the restaurant as the confused manager took notice and looked over with the hostess.

"If I had one wish, one wish in all the world it would be this: marry me," I begged through a thicket of stinging tears. "I love you. I'd do anything to stay with you. Forever." I blinked hot tears down my pale cheeks and drew staccato breaths. Heart pounding, I looked pleadingly into the eyes of the man I truly knew I could not live without. "Please say you'll be my husband. Wylie, I am so, so sorry for everything I have put you through. I love you. I always will. I would do anything, anything at all to get you to love me back again."

Wylie took my hand and pulled me up. He kissed my hand, pulled me into him, and looked into my eyes and whispered, "The tree is happy."

EPILOGUE

Six Months Later

IT ARRIVED THE DAY WYLIE AND I GOT HOME FROM OUR
honeymoon. I hadn't noticed it at first, perched leaning
against the vestibule wall. Sun kissed and high on being
his Mrs., I tossed my duffel onto the floor as Wy and I kissed
good-bye in the doorway for ten minutes until he had to tear
himself off for the restaurant.

"I love you, wife."

I laughed. It still sounded too weird.

"I love you, husband."

He pecked my forehead and ran his hand down my
spine, ending with a little pat on the bum.

I exhaled, flushed and thrilled. It felt so right, no holes,
no regrets, just bliss. I was headed back inside to go call Kira
to tell her we were back on terra firma, when I noticed the
small thin brown box sitting there. I leaned down to pick it
up for Wylie, assuming it was one of his countless Amazon
purchases. But it was addressed in writing I recognized.

Instantly an old familiar feeling washed over me, though
not with the high-tide velocity it once had. Finn. I walked to

the kitchen and found a pair of scissors, which I widened to use as a tape slicer, opening the box. Inside was a copy of his new CD and a piece of folded yellow lined paper:

Dear Hazel,

I hope this finds you well, sweet girl; perhaps it is wrong of me to write to you but I promise this will be my only correspondence as I have no desire to bother you or disrupt your life, which I am sure has brought you back to the lotto-winning Wylie. Since we have last seen each other, I want you to know I have enjoyed the most prolific months of my career. I holed up in Kyoto for a while, dealing with a lot of stuff/demons and getting count-less tracks down for the new album, which you'll find enclosed. The songs are far more layered and nuanced than ever before and for that I have you to thank; your observations and comments on the music were beyond inspiring to me, and even in your absence, your ghost remains my muse. Please don't be alarmed when you listen to my first single, track #1, "Bewitched"—I'm not so sad anymore and rather than feeling steeped in dark-ness, I now find your presence in my life, albeit too short and cometlike, made my world (though still twisted and a bit tortured) a brighter planet. Take a listen, enjoy it, and please know that you didn't do anything wrong by exploring that path with me. I know your life in New York is exactly where it needs to be, and I don't want you to ever be haunted by guilt about Wylie when you jumped off his path to wander my twisted one for

*a few paces. I know you said you felt awful about
the way you treated him by running off with me.
You told me you feared it would leave a little black
dot on your formerly squeaky-clean conscience.
But life is only mastered through those devia-
tions from the well-trodden appointed roadways.
And Hazel, look closer. It's not a dot. It's a heart.*

With love always, FS

With tears spilling from my tired eyes, I opened the
jewel case and popped the CD in my stereo, hitting play
as I plopped on the floor next to it, hugging my knees as I
waited. First was the slow, edgy beat, echoed with a background noise not unlike tearing newspaper. Then, ever so
lightly, the rockified strings of a violin entered. He was right,
each new instrument tiptoed lightly from the wings onto the
song's center stage, rich and textured, lilting yet passion-
punched. I felt like Salieri dissecting and marveling over
each of Mozart's added string or piano keys in *Amadeus*.
But the maestro didn't have lyrics to melt over. I did.

Bewitched

*Just when I thought my core was coal
Reach down my throat into my soul
The thundering clouds were gray and thick
You weren't coy, I wasn't slick.
You poured yourself within the cracks
I didn't know were forming there
I ran my hand along your back
As my blood lusted not to care*

Chorus:
I cannot kiss your mouth, so I'll kiss your heart
I cannot kiss your mouth, so I'll kiss your heart
Bewitched is what I was
Bewitched is what I was
From the very start.

My enchanted blood grew clotted
My once-cold voice I found all knotted
You cast your magic, tragic spell
You dipped your hands in my black well
I'd cherish you always if I could
The empty cutout where you stood

Intrigued you laughed, in guilt you wept
The empty arms where you once slept
Are wound round nothing now but mist
On London streets where we once kissed.

Bridge:
My skin will never forget your touch
My lungs will never forget those breaths
My brain's imprinted with you so much,
Good-bye's a stone garden of little deaths.

I cannot kiss your mouth, so I'll kiss your heart
I cannot kiss your mouth, so I'll kiss your heart
Bewitched is what I was
Bewitched is what I was
From the very start.

"It would never have lasted, you know," Kira said
behind me.

She had let herself in and knelt down beside me.

"I know," I whispered, choked with tears.

"He doesn't want kids. He loves the road. You are the most homebody person I know."

"I know."

"Then why are you crying, honey?"

"Because you're right. Wylie is the love of my life, and only by experiencing the sheer panic of losing him could I realize that, so I don't have any doubts. I'm crying because I feel so lucky. I only got the clarity by living my fantasy. And then the loss of my reality, my rock, my Wylie, was scarier than that plummeting plane."

"You're lucky, sweetie. Now you will always know you did the right thing."

"I always thought life was so black and white, like Finn does—love, hate, lust, disgust. Now I know there are so many shades of gray," I said, wiping my very last tear from my now-dry cheek. "This whole year made me a better person, hopefully a better wife."

"It has and it will. Life is long, Hazel. Everyone says how short it is, but life is long. And now in your private moments in your marriage you'll have this. This journey, that song, those memories. And it will always remind you of who you are. When you're forty, when you're fifty, or when you're fat and pregnant with stretch marks or when your boobs are on your waist or when you are graying and wrinkly, you will always know you inspired art. Music that will inspire so many people, the way it did us."

I smiled, grateful for everything. "Who knew one thunderstorm would change the course of my life?"

"Who knows anything, Hazel?" She laughed, shrugging. "That's life."

"That is life," I echoed, leaning back against the foot of

the couch. "Filled with chance and mathematically impossible encounters."

Kira hugged me and welcomed me home and we sipped the iced coffees she'd brought for us.

"I gotta go get the girls," she said, looking at her watch. "I'm glad you're back."

"Me, too," I said. "I love you."

"I love you, too."

My sister and I hugged by the door and when I closed it behind her, I sat on the floor by myself and reread Finn's letter. I stood up, walked to my bedroom, where I took down a large jewelry box from my closet where I saved meaningful cards and letters through the years, and put it at the very bottom of the ribbon-tied pile. I closed the box and put it back up on the top shelf of my closet. I went to sit by the window, not yet ready to deal with unpacking my suitcases. As I looked at the glittering New York vista of lights and backlit water towers and building tops, I unknowingly put my fingertips to the heart-shaped locket around my neck.

It had been empty when Finn had put his lips to the gold.

But now it wasn't.

On our honeymoon, one night Wylie and I decided to take a walk on the beach late at night. The days were so hot that the evening air and cold waves on our feet were heaven. To my surprise, Wylie stopped and knelt down in the water, his pants wet with waves.

"Hazel," he said, looking up at me, "you were the one who proposed, so I didn't get to have my knight-in-shining-armor moment," he said. "But I'm so happy. I'm the luckiest guy in the world that you are my wife."

I blinked back tears, still guilty about everything I'd put him through and was overwhelmed with love for him.

"No, I'm the lucky one," I said. "You were always sure,

you always believed in us. You named your restaurant for me. You had faith before I did, and now I swear to you, I'll never ever waver again."

"Good." He nodded.

"Never ever," I vowed, blinking back tears.

"I think, my Mrs., that it's time to do something."

He reached down and pinched some sand from the beach, then stood up and opened my locket. He put the grains of sand inside and closed it, snapping it shut with a click. Then he leaned in and kissed it.

He took my face in his hands, and kissed me. And it was the most passionate, beautiful kiss of my life. I'd mistaken Finn's dramatic passion and fingers pressed into my back as some sort of purity, but there was no love as rich and perfect as the one my husband and I shared, after everything, on that beach, waves crashing around us.

Remembering that ocean-side moment, I looked at the darkening sky in New York. I felt my locket, recalling Wylie's honeymoon gesture, and that second in time I knew: finally, my heart was full.

CPSIA information can be obtained
at www.ICGtesting.com
Printed in the USA
LVHW032121200122
708831LV00014B/1785